FIZZYBREW AND FEAR

Tales of the Terran Confederacy Book Three

Ralts Bloodthorne

Peeper Corner Publishing

ISBN-13: 9798501177987
ISBN-10: 1477123456

Cover design by: Art Painter
Library of Congress Control Number: 2018675309
Printed in the United States of America

CONTENTS

To many many people, too many to count.

Most of all, to my daughters, who are my biggest fans.

*And to my son, who rose to the challenge and became
a good father, which is what really matters.*

INTRODUCTION

Fizzybrew and Fear is the Third Book of the Tales of the Terran Confederacy, this time featuring Dambree in her very own novella.

There are some corrections, some slight filling out, but otherwise it is pretty much identical to the original text of Reddit.

This will be reprinted in the compiled books as well as the eventual omnibus.

PREFACE

Back when I was 11 or 12 years old, on a bright summer's day, I found a stack of books at a yard sale for a nickle each. I only had a quarter, but the person sold them to me anyway.

My mother hated the books, took them away, my father gave them back, telling her I was old enough to read them.

And I was introduced to Mickey Spillane's Mike Hammer. A hard boiled tough detective forged in the hell of the Pacific Campaign of WW2, in the mean streets of New York City.

There is an homage in this story to *The Big Kill*, the 5th in the series.

You'll know it when you see it.

PROLOGUE

"Murphy is a stone cold bastard." - Unknown

Atruka leaned back in his chair and stared at the illumination strip of the ceiling. He was supposed to go off shift in little more than an hour and this part of his shift always seemed to last the longest. The space station, in a geosynchronous orbit around Hesstla, was responsible for all of the space traffic within the system. Before the Terrans had arrived a little over a year ago, chasing a Unified Corporate Military Fleet, the most he had been required to handle were transports and the odd Corporate Executive runner.

The Precursor Autonomous War Machines had arrived, driving in-system, attacking the orbital and system facilities. Atruka had rode out the fighting in the space station, sweating through his fur, watching in horror as within hours most of the outer-system facilities were destroyed.

With a roar of **HEAVY METAL IS HERE!** the Terran war machine had arrived, striking quickly at the Precursor machines. The majority of the Precursor machines had been destroyed outside the high orbitals, but a few had gotten through to the ground.

The Terrans had landed right afterwards, with fire and ferocity, destroying the Precursor machines on the ground before the Lanaktallan who made up the government could figure out what to do about the killer robots.

Their decision, which Atruka felt would go down in history as one of the worst in the system's history, was to suddenly turn on the Terran military fleet.

Well, that was when the Terrans had crushed the Corporate Military Fleet, the Executor Fleet, the Military Fleet, and had landed on the planet to take the fight to the Overseers.

Atruka had learned that the Lanaktallan had picked a fight with the big primates and the big primates had basically caved their skulls in.

Personally, Atruka appreciated the Terrans. He had been born in debt and had only accrued more debt as life went on. At first, he, like many others, tried to live frugally. Then he had learned, like so many others, that the closer you got to zeroing out your balance the more fees seemed to rack up.

So, he had given up and bought himself training and gotten himself assigned to System Traffic Station Prime, where at least he could relax.

When the Terrans had shown up, they'd dumped the debt files straight into the shredder.

That alone made Atruka willing to support the Terrans.

Then came the massive Terran fleets that brought supplies, fabrication units, and the job of being a fifth assistant system traffic controller had suddenly become a pretty busy job. Things had slowed down in the past few months, however, and boring spots had begun to creep into his shift.

His supervisor, a female Hesstlin named Prektanna, moved over next to him. "Start running scans. They should be cleared but doublecheck and then clear the orbitals around the planet."

Atruka frowned. "There's nothing scheduled and the outer arrays haven't picked up anything coming in on the resonance zone. I don't have any scheduled arrivals."

She shook her head. "Not my idea, came from higher up. They want you to do inner system scans, see if there's any unregistered ships out there."

Atruka sighed. Another pirate sweep. He sat up straight and began querying his boards. Nothing. Nothing. More nothing. Oh, look, nothing. What's that over there? Why, it's nothing. How about over...

His boards suddenly lit up as first a handful then dozens of signatures lit off. Anomalous energy readings, energy flares, the bright lights of heavy power systems. More and more kept coming in.

Atruka leaned over and hit the emergency button. It beeped three times but the sirens didn't sound. He looked up at Prektanna, who was touching her implant and nodding. When she saw him staring at her she shook her head.

"Military drill. It's the Terran Space Force, they're integrating a major military unit with a new power armor regiment," she said. She breathed a sigh of relief. "Supposedly it's Task Force Tiamat, commanded by Admiral Karen Grwarga Thennis of the Terran Space Force."

"Are you sure?" Atruka asked, looking at his monitors. Even more pinpoints were showing up and most of the newly arrived craft were moving toward Hesstla at a high rate of speed and in formations that made his fur stand on end.

"Let me see. Throw it up on the big screen," Prektanna said. When he did so she stared at it. "Get me a scan of those ships. This doesn't look right."

Istalup made a motion of assent and hit his scanners.

The return signal was immediate and terrifying.

YOU BELONG TO US! bellowed out, making that space station ring. Several beings collapsed, two had seizures, and Atruka hit the medical alert.

"That's not the Terrans!" Atruka said, blood running from his nose and his vision blurry.

Prektanna looked up from the floor and coughed blood that had run into her mouth from her sinuses.

Atruka knew he shouldn't do it, that all of his training told him to keep his hands off that button.

Instead, he pulled out his physical key, unlocked the clear armaplas casing, flipped it up, and slapped the big red button.

Sirens began to howl and the lights went to a dull red. The empty station that nobody ever sat at since the Terrans installed it suddenly had all the monitors go live. Atruka saw that battle-screens were spinning up, point defense was going live, and psychic shielding was being engaged.

"Signal the Terrans! Tell them we're under attack!" Prektanna yelled, pulling herself up. She looked at the communications station and saw the being that normally manned it was unconscious, bleeding from the ears and nose and mouth, foam drooling out of the slack mouth. She staggered over and started trying to contact the Terrans.

This time the roar of "You Belong to Us!" was quieter and didn't claw at the mind.

Atruka saw that the Terran military bases just demanded all the airspace above them and around them for twenty miles at ground level be cleared in a cone that reached up to orbit in a thousand mile diameter.

"Task Force Tiamat, this is Belvak-8, we're under attack by Precursor forces in strength!" Prektanna said, wiping the blood from her face. "I say again, we are under attack by Precursor forces in strength!"

Atruka was busy ordering every ship in the system to flee immediately.

The station shuddered as something slammed into the battlescreens.

"Task Force Tiamat, this is Orbital Control, Belvak-8, we are under attack by Precursor forces in strength!" Prektanna said. "Please respond!"

HEAVY METAL INCOMING! roared out from the speakers.

Atruka's display flashed that he had an incoming transmission. He brought it up and froze.

It was less than a minute before the Terrans would arrive. They would break off if he gave the signal, but the cleared areas he'd been tasked with clearing out in the beginning of his shift were about to get a lot of really big ships arriving.

"They're coming in inside the Resonance Zone," Atruka said softly, his fur between his ears, down the back of his head, and along his spine raising up in shock.

"Task Force Tiamat, please respond! There are Precursor vessels in orbit! Break off! Break off!" Prektanna shouted. "Task Force Tiamat, please respond!"

HEAVY METAL INCOMING!

Atruka was frozen. He had less than thirty seconds to do

something before the Terrans hit the point of no return. They were going to come in right on top the Precursors that were flooding the orbitals according to the coordinates, coming in on a tight vector that would end with a complete stop.

"Task Force Tiamat, please... I'm on the wrong channel! Oh, Oh, what channel?" Prektanna said. She reached down and grabbed the unconscious technician. "What's the frequency, Ken'nth?"

HEAVY METAL IS HERE!

Atruka stared at his screen in horror as the first units of the Terran Task Force Tiamat streaked into existence, their ships sliding between the Precursor vessels that were already shedding landing units onto the planet's surface.

HEAVY METAL INCOMING! sounded again and Atruka looked at his monitor.

More ships were incoming.

Working frantically he sent instructions to deploy further away, away from the Precursor machines. Each time the call of **HEAVY METAL INCOMING!** came he returned emergency redirect coordinates. He tried to keep them near the planet, away from the Precursors.

The main display stopped showing the orbitals and a Terran female in an armored vacuum suit appeared, laying back in a reclining shock cradle.

"What in the name of the Digital Omnimessiah's glittering ballsack is going on, Hesstla-Orbital?" she asked.

"WE'RE UNDER ATTACK!" Prektanna screamed as the station shuddered again. Somewhere far away a klaxon began to wail.

"Coms! All ships!" the Terran female snapped. She looked right back at the camera as a long stream of suddenly connected ships scrolled down the side of the image. "HOT ZONE HOT ZONE HOT ZONE! THIS IS NOT A DRILL! SHIELDS UP! GUNS CLEAR! RUN THE HASH!"

She looked at the three still moving beings in the control room. "Well, now we know that your hyperpulse generator didn't get the right codes loaded. We're coming in, give us a pair of two light second diameter bubble two light minutes from the planet on either side, we'll come in there."

Atruka frantically did as she asked, putting it on the other side of the larger moon and then on the opposite side of the planet. His computer crunched the numbers and as soon as his panel beeped, much much much faster than his old panel could have, he slapped the button and send the coordinates.

The Terran female looked at them through the screen. "Hold the Line, Brothers, the Hamburger Kingdom's Hammer is coming."

The screen blanked.

Prektanna hung her head and started weeping as the station shuddered again. "It was supposed to just be training. Just training."

Atruka didn't answer.

He was too busy putting small bubbles around his home planet for ships to exit hyperspace into.

TASK FORCE TIAMAT

HOT ZONE HOT ZONE HOT ZONE!

BELVAK-8 UNDER PRECURSOR ATTACK!

GO TO LOCAL COMMAND!

SHIELDS UP! GUNS FREE! RUN THE HASH!

YOU KNOW WHAT TO DO!

-Admiral Thennis, Commanding

SECOND TELKAN MARINE DIVISION

ALL UNITS GO TO LOCAL COMMAND!

HOLD WHAT YOU GOT!

WE BRING THE FUN!

III CORPS

Hit the planet. Rapid reload on the Clone Banks. Precursor's are on the ground, people.

Bring down the Hamburger Kingdom's Hammer on those metal

bastards!
Protect civilians.

FIRST CAVALRY DIVISION

You know what to do, men.

SECOND ARMOR DIVISION

Enemy has landed in force.
Regroup when possible.

FIRST INFANTRY DIVISION

LETTUM HAVVIT BOYS!

FIFTH MECH DIVISION

Precursor forces in strength. Orbital drops.
Engage and destroy.
WE ARE THE METAL!

...*Billy Carriage*, do you read? We have you on visual. Do you read? *Billy Carriage*, do you read?...

MAKE-OUT POINT
& MADNESS

*"The universe will hurt you, beat you, and
think it's funny."* – Terran Saying

Dambree left the house, through the window as one was wont to do when avoiding a parental unit's notice, and snuck across the yard. She jumped over the short fence and hurried down the alley. She was dressed in soft cloth, a pair of soft pants made of blue cloth, a shirt of blue that had short sleeves and left her belly-fur exposed, and a pair of soft shoes. In the last year she had seen the Overseers flee the system and leave the entire world empty of their presence, then the hairless primates called "Terrans" showed up and wanted to do trade, wanted to be part of Hesstla society. They had begun teaching at schools, working in stores, and slowly visiting the planet.

It had been an exciting, heady time, and she had loved every moment of it.

Over the summer she had met a male Hesstlin named Alkree, and despite her male parental unit's admonitions of 'no daughter of mine...' regards dating, she had still carried on through private chats and messages. Alkree was handsome, older, and had a ground vehicle and a job overseeing agricultural robots.

That's why Dambree was sneaking out to meet him even though her parental units would disapprove of her sneaking out at night, her bare midriff, and the fur dye she had on her cheeks and the tips of her ears.

She exited the alley and walked to the corner, waiting for Alkree just like they had agreed. She checked her datapad and saw that Alkree had left a message that he was on his way.

I'm here she sent back.

After a few minutes Alkree pulled up in his ground car. A black car with narrow headlights and a roomy passenger cabin. Alkree popped open the door and she slid into the car, looking at him. He was tall, lanky, with a stripe of shaved fur on the top of his head and down his neck. He had metal piercings in his ears and had dyed the tips of his ears, around his eyes, and the tip of his nose black. He leaned over and licked the side of her neck and face, making her giggle, then handed her a bottle. She opened it and sniffed at it. Uddlevent fruit liquor.

"Thank you," she said, sipping it lightly. She handed it back and he bumped noses with her before taking a long drink off the bottle.

"Where are we going?" she asked.

"How does Shalpeenea Bluff sound to you?" Alkree said, turning smoothly onto the side-road.

Dambree nodded, taking another sip of the alcohol and gulping. The Bluff overlooked the agricultural fields and the city both and was a well-known spot for boyfriends to take their girlfriends. The thought made her fur prickle just to think about it.

Alkree put his hand on her thigh and she giggled as he rubbed the soft cloth up and down her leg. The car moved up the incline up to the bluff as she sipped at the sweet liquor, taking three or four sips for every drink that Alkree took.

She was feeling a little lightheaded and tingly across her ears and face when Alkree parked the car so that they could see the robotic tenders in the agricultural fields below and the lights of the city beyond.

The evening was giddy for Dambree, the attention that the older Alkree was paying to her, the lights of the city beyond and the robots moving through the fields, and the alcohol all combined to make her head swim.

Faintly, in the distance, through the alcohol buzz and the euphoria of Alkree's attention, she heard someone yell something about belonging to them, but she closed her eyes and sighed deeply. Alkree was guiding her to lay back in the seat, helping her clumsy fingers.

She was looking up through the windshield when she saw the streaks of light in the sky. A few, then dozens, then hundreds. She moved her head, looking closer, as the streaks seemed to slice across the indigo night sky. Her arms were over her head, out the side window, and her shirt bunched up under her armpits and against her throat. Some of them were at weird angles, where the streak disappeared and only a slowly growing point of light was visible. Alkree took that time to pull her shirt off over her head, tossing it into the passenger seat beside him, and when she looked up even more shooting stars had started. There were bright sparks erupting to life in the sky that quickly went away, clusters of them, of all different colors.

"Shooting stars," she said, starting to sit up. Alkree moved his head, cursing, as she turned in place, shuffling her knees because her pants were down around them, and stuck her head out the open window. She laughed, feeling light headed, and opened the door, kicking out of her pants as she climbed out of the car and looked at the night sky.

HEAVY METAL INCOMING! roared out from every flat surface, every speaker. Many people winced, a few cried out in fear and confusion and pain.

Alkree mumbled something and followed her as she stared up at the sky.

She wasn't the only one. Several vehicles' couples had gotten out, although most of them were fully dressed, all staring at the sky and pointing at the streaks, the twinkling of sparks in the sky, or the steadily growing bright dots that were seemingly dropping down.

"Get back in the car," Alkree said, pulling on her arm.

She pulled away, pointing at one of the bright dots. "What do you think it is?"

"Who cares?" Alkree said. He grabbed her arm and pulled at her again. "Come on."

One of the balls of light suddenly *streaked* forward, roaring over the cars, making all the Hesstlin duck and scream. It hit in the trees right behind, a ball of fire reaching up to the sky and the impact making the trees wave back and forth.

Hesstlin were yelling, wondering what it was, wondering where it came from, some wanted to run toward it, some wanted to leave right away.

Alkree adjusted his black vest and stepped toward the woods. "I'm going to go see who crashed a flitter," he said, looking over his shoulder. "Unless you can think of something better to do."

She shook her head, looking back up. She lifted the bottle to her mouth and took another sip of the liquor, the movement absent minded as she watched streaks pass straight over them. She looked back in time to see Alkree and some other males and females go into the woods. She sighed and looked up as she took another drink, flickering her ears nervously.

HEAVY METAL IS HERE! roared out over the speakers and from all around.

More bright flashes appeared up in the air. She squinted, trying to make them out. After a minute she looked down and saw her pants laying behind the car. Suddenly reminded she was outside in her underwear she moved over and bent over to grab her pants, laughing as she almost went headfirst into the ground.

There was a loud groaning noise that vibrated the air, so loud, deep bass she could feel vibrating her bones. It was followed by the snapping of wood and bright searchlights began to sweep the woods, casting shadows on the vehicles.

One male Hesstlin and his girlfriend got in their car and took off, leaving behind a cloud of dust.

There was a bright red light and screaming sounded from the woods.

She turned around in time to see several Hesstlin run from the woods, screaming. One was a female holding onto the stump of an arm. She got to the car, stumbling and whining, and the male helped her into the car.

Cars were starting up as Dambree looked around.

"Alkree?" she called out, suddenly nervous.

There was more bright red flashes and trees started cracking, falling to the side, and even more floodlights began to pan around the forest.

The male Hesstlin ran out of the woods, tripping and falling when he tried to jump the ditch and misjudged the distance. He scrambled up to her, his vest torn, a couple of his metal studs torn from his ears. His eyes were wild and it was obvious he was panicked.

Dambree looked up as a bright light suddenly shone down from the heavens in flash. She saw a spreading light in the sky that slowly went out, staring at it befuddled, wondering what it was.

Alkree grabbed her, pulling at her. "Get in car, you stupid pup," he shrieked.

Dambree yanked back, her eyes filling with tears from his tone and his words. There was a crashing of breaking wood behind her but she was staring at Alkree with her eyes wide with hurt.

Alkree's eyes somehow widened even further in horror. He stepped up to Dambree and grabbed her, backing up, holding her at arm's length, his hands tight enough around her upper arms that it made her cry out in pain.

"Not me! Not me!" Alkree screamed. A bright red line went up and down Alkree's face and Dambree could see it on the back of her arms.

Dambree's foot hit a rock and she cried out, crumpling as her leg collapsed. She looked up just in time to see it happen.

A long tentacle with five graspers around the end snaked over the top of her, the tentacles made of dark metal, ringed every handspan or so, and the end of the tentacle settled on Alkree's head. The graspers flipped down, holding his head securely.

Alkree screamed and there was a crunching sound that reminded Dambree of a food chopper trying to digest a large thick tuber. She stared as his screaming turned to gurgles and suddenly his eyes sucked into his head. The graspers let Alkree go and he fell silently to the ground.

She realized that the top of his head was gone, to reveal an empty skull slicked with blood.

She rolled over and looked up, her eyes widening.

The thing stood on six stilts, ringed metal legs with wide flat pads on the ground. It was a wide oval, three stilts per side, and had rough looking mechanical sections on top. There was a dozen glass or plasteel or crysteel bubbles on the top, machinery visible inside. Three of them were blue, lit up, and she could see what looked like brains with tubes and rods and wires stuck in them. One of the dark glass bubbles lit up with soft white light, revealing bubbling liquid, rods, crystals, wires, and other devices inside.

The big machine vibrated, the tentacle pulling back and retracting into the flat black oval at the base. Dambree scrambled backwards, over Alkree, not even noticing as a red light came on, flashing, and a red line went down her body.

The red line suddenly widened into a grid and she blinked as the red light in her eyes suddenly flashed.

HEAVY METAL IS HERE! Suddenly thundered from every surface, from every speaker.

The machine shuddered and Dambree saw a brain lifted up on a black metal rod as thick as her wrist. The tubes, wires, rods, and other things suddenly stuck into the brain and the machine shuddered again.

Her head hit the car door as the rod retracted from the bottom of the brain and the crysteel glass globe suddenly lit with a blue light.

She suddenly *knew* what was going to happen to her as she kicked her feet. Dambree turned, climbing into the car, sobbing to herself.

Around her every other Hesstlin was getting into their cars as four more of the stilted machines came out of the woods. Something larger, much larger, in the woods, let out the loud bass cry, making the metal and plastic of the vehicles vibrate.

The windshield shattered onto Dambree as she sat up in the driver's seat. The keys were still in so that the satellite music player could keep going. It was only giving out atonal shrieks, warbling up and down the scales in a random order. She started the car, put it in reverse, and hit the gas.

The tentacle, reaching for her, smashed the door off with the scream of tearing metal and the clatter of shattering plexglass and plasteel. The car hit the stilted machine, not budging the machine, and she threw it in forward, hitting the accelerator.

The little car whirred, the batteries driving the electric motor, as she turned onto the road, her foot holding the accelerator to the floor. She looked behind her as lights shined in the back window. At least three ground-cars were behind her. She saw an aircar take off only to be destroyed by a bright streak that turned the aircar into debris falling from a ball of fire.

Someone slammed their car into the door-less driver's side of hers. A tentacle reached out, punched through the roof of the car that had just pushed hers to the side, and yanked the female passenger out, pulling her screaming into the darkness.

Dambree was weeping as she slammed the other car back, then, at the bottom of the incline, made a hard turn into the agricultural field, pushing the car through the stalks of mellitgrain. She looked behind her and saw at least four of the stilted machines chasing the cars that were still fleeing the bluff.

Panicked, she slapped off the lights, uncaring if she hit something in the dark. She couldn't see through the stalks anyway, they were slapping against the hood and vanishing under the body. The car was bouncing and jostling, alarms ringing from the dash, warning her she wasn't on a recognized road.

She looked behind her and saw it.

The big one.

It was at least six stories high, heaving itself up on hundreds of insect legs. It had segmented eyes that glowed purple, its jaws covered by mechanical tentacles that whipped around in a frenzy and bearded by more insectile legs. It had what looked like greasy looking blisters that, as she watched, two flying machines crawled from and fluttered their legs, drying the metal and crystal of their wings and carapace.

Whimpering, she looked forward, trying to ignore the immense bass roar from the huge machine.

YOU BELONG TO ME roared out in her head and she winced, crying out, as pain spiked through her head at the authoritative words.

Faintly, dimly, she heard another voice. This one raised in wrath and defiance.

EAT A DICK! she heard faintly.

She drove through the stalks, in the dark, whimpering, wiping blood from her nose, as she sped away from the site where only moments before she had been sighing and trembling as Alkree had made her body feel new things she'd never dreamed of.

Dambree saw the flask of alcohol rocking back and forth on the seat and reached out with one hand, pawing at it, until she managed to get it. She ripped the cap off with her teeth and took a drink.

Not a sip.

Three long swallows.

She wiped her mouth as the car bounced onto the road. She yanked the wheel, the wheels slid out, she overcorrected, then overcorrected again. The car spun in a circle and she managed to get it back onto the road before she drove too far half in the mellintgrain.

She kept the pedal to the floor, the wind, colder now, blasting in through the windshield, through the empty doorframe. The car kept beeping, warning her she was going too fast, as she pushed it almost to fifty miles an hour. She screamed and pounded on the dash when it slowed her back down to a safe thirty. She could see cars ahead of her, heading out of the city, out of the suburbs, and cars behind her, following her into the city.

The woodline of the Bluff was on fire.

HEAVY METAL IS HERE! sounded out again and sparks shot from the dash.

Dambree looked up from the dash just as a low flying aircraft shot by her. Lasers pulsed from the bottom, white with a red core, and the vehicles in front of her exploded.

Dambree hammered on the dash more and the car rewarded

her by having the warning cut off with a squawk and the electric engine humming faster.

She was almost up to fifty miles an hour again when several more low-flying aircraft roared overhead. These ones didn't shoot, instead the slowed down, turned around, and matched speed with the cars behind her. As she glanced behind her and looked, tentacles slammed through the roofs of the cars, pulling out the screaming occupants.

She could see blue flashes as crysteel globes on the top of the vehicle, mostly hidden by crude looking armor and mechanical parts, started lighting up with an interior blue glow.

Crying, she swerved onto her street. Two machines were tearing into houses, pulling the screaming Hesstlin from their hiding places. The screams stopping, the graspers opening, the bodies falling, and steam rising from their emptied skulls as the bodies crumpled onto the carefully manicured lawns.

She didn't bother with the driveway, driving right up on the lawn. She left the engine running as she jumped out, running to the house. The door was locked and she hammered on it.

Five houses behind her a machine started ripping into the roof.

"MOM! DAD! OPEN THE DOOR!" she screamed.

Someone screamed as they were dragged from inside the closet. A body pulled from beneath the bed was released to fall to the lawn with an empty skull.

Crying she moved to the middle of the lawn, ran forward, and threw herself, shoulder first, against the plas door. It shattered around her and she ran into the house.

"MOM! DAD!" she screamed again.

Her mother came out, peeking around the corner.

"We have to leave! Now! Come on!" Dambree screamed.

Her mother, her ears flat against her head and her eyes wide with horror, shook her head, her mouth moving with no sound.

Dambree ran forward, grabbing her mother's arm, and did something she would have never ever thought of, in all her long fourteen years of life, before this night.

She slapped her mother.

Hard.

"GET THE LITTLES!" Dambree screamed.

She didn't know she was mostly deaf.

Her mother scampered away, yanking over the bedroom door. Dambree followed her, seeing her little sister under the bed. She grabbed her sister by the hair when her sister tried to pull back, dragging her screaming sibling out from under the bed.

Her mother had her youngest sister and her little brother by their pajamas, standing in the middle of the room, staring at her daughter, who was only wearing her waist and groin modesty clothing.

"LET'S GO!" Dambree yelled, thinking she was speaking normally.

Her mother mouthed something, but Dambree was already running.

Two stilters across the street were tearing into a house only two down from Dambree's. Directly across the street two fliers were tearing apart the roof.

"DON'T LOOK!" Dambree yelled, physically throwing her little sister through the empty windowframe and into the back seat. She turned and grabbed her baby sister from her mother, repeating the action, then again for her little brother.

"GET ON THE FLOOR! COVER YOUR HEADS!" she yelled. She ran around to the driver's side and slid behind the wheel.

Her father stood on the grass, staring at her. The inside of his long ears were pink with anger at seeing his daughter unclad.

"GET IN!" Dambree yelled.

Her father shook his head, mouthing words. Her mother was mouthing words, pointing at her own groin then at Dambree.

A tentacle came down, grabbing her father, lifting him up.

Dambree's mother jumped through the empty window frame and into the vehicle.

Dambree hammered down the pedal, punching the car into forward, and sprayed grass as she pulled a sliding curve back onto the street.

A tentacle tore a hole in the roof but missed anything else.

More streaks were coming down from the sky, which was lit up with flashes and streaks of light. They punched through sky, burning their way to the ground.

Dambree didn't care, she just kept her foot on the accelerator.

YOU BELONG TO ME! rang out in her head.

Her siblings cried out in pain and fear. Her mother clutched her head and cried out.

Dambree screamed with the reply.

EAT A DICK!

The car sped into the night.

THE MADNESS OF
THE LEMURS

"Victory or Death, Either is Fine" – Terran Motto

"Civil Defense is reporting thousands of landings planet-wide. All civilians are urged to get to public shelters or, barring that, basements and other underground shelters. Terran military forces urge all Hesstlin within twenty miles of a Terran military base to seek refuge at the base," the voice was saying over the radio. The woman's voice was shot with static and the loud ka-rack of laser weaponry and the high pitched whine of autocannons could be heard in the background. "Terran military forces have labeled these things Type IV Precursors. They have entered the city and are attacking citizens."

Dambree wept silently as she drove the car on the road, following the vehicles fleeing the city. Unlike the other vehicles, she had the lights off. Her mother was beside her, holding her baby sister, who was nursing. The baby's eyes were red and her fur was damp with tears from being pulled from her bed and thrown unceremoniously into the back of a car.

"You left your father," her mother said softly as the cars came to a stop again. People began honking.

"He was dead," Dambree said, her voice flat.

In her mind rose up the image of Alkree's eyes being sucked into his skull as the tentacle vacuumed his brain from his skull. How the blood-slicked bone interior of his skull steamed in the cool night air.

How he had evacuated his bladder and bowels in death as she had scrambled over his body.

"Steer clear of any landing forces. Terran forces are under attack even as they attempt to make planetfall. Do not approach any landing forces," the female said. "I repeat: Civil Defense is reporting thousands..."

Dambree reached over and slapped the button on the radio, shutting it off.

The cars moved forward a few feet.

A flier roared overhead, sliding to a stop. Tentacles came down, tearing open the roof of the car beneath it. The half-dozen crysteel orbs two-thirds buried in armor and machinery had only one that glowed softly blue. The tentacles pulled three Hesstlin from the car. They were screaming as the tentacle lifted them up.

Doors burst open as Hesstlin fled their vehicles and up or down the highway, screaming, to get away from the flier.

Dambree's mother reached for the door and Dambree reached out and grabbed the fur between her mother's ear, yanking her back in the car as her mother screamed in pain.

"STAY IN THE CAR!" Dambree yelled, slamming her mother into the seat. The baby didn't lose suction on the nipple.

YOU BELONG TO ME roared out in her head as the flier dropped all three limp bodies. Three of the orbs went from dark to softly glowing white. Dambree knew they'd go blue in only a few moments as the flier roared off.

"EAT A DICK!" Dambree screamed, echoing the voice that had answered each bellow. It was stronger now, more voices joining in, echoing in her mind. They were defiant, angry, furious, and she felt stronger joining them in their defiance.

Dambree cranked the wheel and hit the accelerator, bouncing the car over the curbs and into the field of ullikleaf.

"What's a dick?" her mother asked, rubbing the back of her head. The baby was holding tight to her breast with both hands, still nursing.

"I don't know," Dambree admitted, gritting her teeth and trying to keep the wheel straight. "I don't care."

"You shouldn't leave the road," her mother said.

"I know," Dambree said. The car hit a furrow and jostled

heavy.

The baby glared at Dambree.

"I peed myself, mommy," Dambree's little sister said. "And my head hurts from Dambree pulling my hair."

"You shouldn't pull your sister's hair," Dambree's mother said.

"I know," Dambree said. Her shoulder hurt from where she had crashed into the door. It felt like there was something inside grinding, like marbles or something. Her fingers tingled and her biceps hurt.

"You aren't old enough to drive," Dambree's mother noted.

"I know," Dambree said.

"You are only in your lower modesty clothing. People can see your mammaries," her mother said.

"I know."

"Your makeup looks like a prostitute," her mother said.

"I KNOW!" Dambree half screamed, tears running from her eyes.

A flier roared by overhead, close enough it rocked the car. There were two others with it, dark machines with a faint blue glow on the top.

Swallowing thickly, Dambree looked in the passenger side rearview mirror, the only one left.

Another flier was chasing them. A crude looking craft of black metal that looked somehow wet as well as corroded and badly welded. It had streaks erupting from the nose, arcing in on the left-hand flier. The crashing roar of repeated detonations slapped Dambree's ears right before the aircraft roared overhead.

She saw the armored hand crushing a planet of the Terran Space Force on the bottom of the wings.

"They shouldn't fly so low," her mother noted.

"I KNOW!" she yelled, slamming the brakes. The car jerked to stop and her siblings in the back seat cried out. She turned to her mother, resisting the urge to grab the older Hesstlin and shake her. "I KNOW! I GOT THE CONCEPT! DAMBREE BAD!"

She turned back to facing out the windshield. "Now will

you shut up and let me..."

YOU BELONG TO ME!

This time she screamed before the voice had finished shouting in her head.

"EAT A FUCKING DICK!" she screamed as she slammed down the pedal. The electric engine whirred and the car started slowly moving forward, gradually picking up speed.

"That sounds like profanity to me," her mother harumphed.

"I don't care," Dambree said quietly, reaching out and grabbing the bottle from where she'd wedged it. She took two long swallows, emptying it, and threw it out the missing door.

"Drinking. Cursing. Parading around in your underclothing. Hitting your mother and yelling at her," her mother said, shaking her head and making clicking sounds with her tongue. "How did I ever raise such a daughter."

Dambree slammed on the brakes, turning to look at her mother.

"They are *killing* people out there, and you're going to guilt me? Now? Right now? Right after we saw people get their BRAINS SUCKED OUT?" she yelled.

Her mother slapped her. "Don't you scream at me, Dambree Limberton," her mother said stuffily. She disconnected the baby and set her on the seat then turned to Dambree, shaking one accusing finger. "You need to be more respectful to your..."

The tentacle punched through the roof, the graspers closed on her head, and she was yanked out of the car, still shaking one finger at Dambree.

Dambree slammed on the accelerator again, plowing through the grain, jerking the wheel to the side in the hopes that whatever had just taken her mother couldn't follow her. The car was bouncing across the ruts, through the furrows, slamming down and then bouncing into the air.

Dambree reached out and grabbed her baby sister with one hand, catching her by the leg as she flew up into the air, pulling her onto her lap.

Her sister growled and bit her.

The grain suddenly ended and she shot across a dirt access road.

She could see lightning ripping at the air, explosions in midair. Some kind of wavy curtain made of light in mid-air was barely visible, snapping and sparking at times.

She was across the road and back into the grain, blindly steering for the lightning ripping at the air. She could look up and see streaks whipping from whatever it was and into the sky.

The side of the roof above her ripped open and she screamed, leaning to the side, putting one foot on the steering wheel, pushing the baby onto the floor of the passenger shirt so she was laying on Dambree's abandoned and forgotten shirt.

The tentacle whipped in, the open graspers snapping shut on thin air.

Dambree saw the streaks of light sudden start whipping by the flier.

Then they hit. Explosions cracked out, hurting Dambree's ears, and the flier stopped as if it had ran into the wall, the entire front consumed by rapid explosions.

Part of Dambree noticed it only had one blue light as she sat up and grabbed the steering wheel again. She looked back in time to see it explode with a shriek that she could hear inside her mind and fall into the grain a ball of greasy looking fire.

I love you, Momma, she thought to herself, tears running down her face as she looked forward, her foot holding the accelerator down.

The car hit a rut and bounced onto another dirt road, this one leading sort of toward where the bars of light kept coming from. She cranked the wheel, overturned, then overcorrected, trying to see through her tears. Her baby sister and her siblings in the back seat all squalled as the car rocked back and forth.

She came around the corner and before she could react, she hit an invisible biped in the middle of the road. The surprised looking suddenly no longer invisible biped bounced off the hood, stared at her in shock, and then vanished over the top of the car.

Dambree slammed on the brakes. She got out and looked behind her.

She could faintly make out the biped laying in the dirt. Its clothing kept blurring into the dirt road, making it hard to see. She ran over to it and bent down.

"Oh dear oh dear, I'm sorry, I'm sorry," she cried out, tears running out of her eyes and falling onto the biped's face.

"Fuck, my legs. They're broken," the biped moaned. She could see it had a rifle on a strap attached to its back and a heavy belt with a pistol and round spheres with rings on the top.

There was a low bass roar that trembled the bones.

"Help me to your car," the biped said, holding out its arms. "Drag me. We don't have much time."

She tried, pulling on the bipeds arms, but she couldn't move it.

"You're too heavy. I'm sorry," she said.

The biped looked at her. "Oh, Vat Grown Luke paddling a quasar powered rowboat, you're just a little kid, aren't you?"

Dambree nodded, still crying.

The biped looked past her.

"And you've got kids in the car?" it asked. Dambree thought it was a male as she nodded.

"Well, fuck," it said.

"Fuck?" Dambree said. She squinted, trying to get a good look at the biped's face in the darkness. "Fuck? Fuck! You're a Terran!" she said. "Oh, please, save my siblings, Mister Terran! Please?"

The Terran, who looked so much different than her teachers and the other ones she had seen before this horrible night, looked up and coughed. "I can't, kid. My legs are broken," he sighed. "Move, I'll try to pull myself..."

A stilter chose that moment to burst out of the grain fields. It looked the wrong way at first, then toward Dambree, the Terran, the car, and her siblings.

YOU BELONG TO ME! the stilter roared out into Dambree's mind, making her siblings scream in pain. Its legs extended and it went from only a foot above the ground to nearly ten feet up.

"GET FUCKED!" the Terran yelled back, pulling around the rifle that was on its back.

"EAT A DICK!" Dambree screamed.

The Terran fired, hitting the front leg. The stilter jerked, the leg shattering, and rushed forward. The Terran shifted the rifle even as Dambree cried out, covering her ears, and fired again at the same time as the stilter fired a bluish bolt with a red core that hit the chest of the Terran.

The bluish glowing globe shattered. Then the other. The stilter lurched to the side and the Terran cocked something on the bottom, aimed, and fired the weapon again, this time getting a dull sounding thump.

The top of the stilter exploded and it crashed to the ground.

The Terran was laying on the ground, gasping, his clothing on his chest scorched and smoking. He rolled slightly and coughed, then rolled back.

Dambree grabbed the straps that went from his belt over his shoulders, and screaming as loud as she could, started to drag him backwards toward the car.

Another stilter came out of the grain. Then another.

Like the previous one they looked the wrong way first. The stilts were retracted, collapsed, but Dambree knew when they saw the Terran and Dambree, they would suddenly stand up.

The Terran fumbled at his waist before holding up the pistol. "Security interlock disable, authorization two two niner alpha niner five."

"Disengaged," the pistol said in a female voice.

The two stilters began to turn around.

"Take this, kid. Get out of here. Don't let them corner you. If they do... use it on the littles first, then yourself. Push it against the temple," The Terran gasped.

Dambree let him go, taking the pistol.

The stilters saw them.

YOU BELONG TO

"EAT A FUCKING DICK, STRETCH!" the Terran yelled back,

Dambree mostly joining him.

The two stilters rocked back.

"Run, kid," the Terran said, bringing his rifle around. He glanced at the magazine jutting from the bottom and sighed.

Dambree turned and ran as the Terran started shooting. She dove into the car, looking behind her as she heard and explosion. One of the stilters was falling to the side, the top burning, as the Terran cocked the weapon again.

The second stilter rushed him.

Dambree looked at the pistol. It had a red button that she pushed and it turned green. The weapon somehow felt heavier in her hand as she carefully wrapped her hand around the grip.

The Terran was shooting.

She raised the pistol, climbing half over the seat and looking down.

Her little brother and little sister looked at her, their eyes wide, the fur on their faces wet with tears. Blood had run from their noses and ears.

Beyond them the Terran blocked the first tentacle strike with the rifle.

"I love you," she told her brother.

The Terran blocked the second strike but it yanked the rifle away even as two other tentacles lunged forward. He slapped one away but the second grabbed an arm.

"I want momma," her brother said.

Dambree swallowed thickly. "Do you want to see her again?" she asked.

The Terran smacked away the second tentacle but a third grabbed his other arm.

Her siblings nodded.

"Close your eyes," she said softly, watching as the Terran was lifted up, looking at both of her siblings who were on either side of the Terran being lifted into the air by his outstretched arms.

They both closed their eyes as the tentacle came down on the Terran's head.

She lifted the pistol, putting it next to her brother's temple.

The tentacles dropped the Terran. One of the globes went white. It had four other blue globes.

She closed her eyes, trying to will herself to press the firing stud.

EAT A FUCKING DICK, YOU METAL COCK SUCKER! EAT ALL THE DICKS! roared out in her mind.

Her brother and sister screamed, clapping their hands to their ears and falling to the floor. The baby began screaming.

Dambree opened her eyes and stared.

YOU THINK I'M INSIDE HERE WITH YOU? YOU'RE IN HERE WITH ME, YOU METAL BRAIN SUCKING LOSER! the Terran was somehow screaming.

Dumbree looked at the Terran. It was limp in the road. She looked up at the stilter.

One of the globes was red. Bright, shining, enraged crimson.

The tentacles came up and began slamming into the other globes.

She didn't know why, but she knew the Terran was somehow doing it. She turned around, sitting back down, and dropped the pistol into her lap as she slammed the accelerator to the floor.

The car whined as it spewed dirt from under the tires, blocking the view of the stilter dancing and capering around even as the tentacles slammed into the crysteel globes.

OLLY OLLY OXEN FREE! COME OUT COME OUT WHEREVER YOU ARE! the Terrans voice shouted. **I SPY, WITH MY LITTLE EYE, SOMETHING THAT BEGINS WITH... BRAIN!**

She was crying again as she rounded the corner, leaving behind the maddened gibbering capering machine.

There was an explosion behind her that lit up the night.

Dambree kept her foot on the pedal, heading toward the wavering wall of light.

They're mad. They're all mad.

FIZZYBREWS, NIBBLES, AND SIPPIES

"Don't ask me how far I'll go to survive, you don't want to know." - Unknown

Dambree wiped her eyes and glanced down at the baby. She was laying on Dambree's shirt, sucking her thumb, glaring at Dambree with her wide amber eyes. Her ears were held tightly against her head in response to the loud yelling that sounded out inside one's head more than it reached the ears. Dambree swerved around blackened and smoking debris in the road, slowing down. Her eyes and face were beginning to hurt from squinting to see through the darkness.

The glittering curtain had moved away, the firing from guns coming to a stop. There had been the rumble of great engines and it had moved away.

That had made Dambree almost start crying.

It wasn't fair. She was almost there when it had driven away, leaving her on a debris filled dirt road driving a car that was barely held together.

The GPS was out, the navigation system was out, and when Dambree had checked, even the headlights were out. She had no idea where she was going, how fast she was going.

She only knew she needed to keep moving.

Which is why she was weaving between massive chunks of burnt and blackened metal. Some of it was sparking deep inside, a few times she saw dead and dismembered bodies, bipeds, all of them, some of them half-clad in armor.

"Keep your heads down, don't look outside," she ordered

her brother and sister.

For once they didn't argue, just shifted so they were laying on the floorboards. They were still whimpering, still frightened from when the Terran had been slorped by the stilter then had somehow taken over part of it and fought itself.

HEAVY METAL INCOMING! roared out and she flinched.

HEAVY METAL IS HERE! roared out right after.

She reached out with one hand, slapping at the radio, and it came on with the high pitched tones of the Civil Defense Authority Emergency Alert System. She flinched but then went back to staring out the broken windshield, weaving between the wreckage.

"...forces are making groundfall and engaging Precursor machines at this time. Terran Defense Forces encourage everyone to seek shelter. Do not approach military units outside of military bases unless you have no other choice. Seek shelter in basement and underground structures. Do not attempt to reach friends of family. Do not attempt to reach any of the Rescue Stations broadcast earlier as they may not be in operation. Clear all roadways. Turn off all lights and electrical devices in the homes by breaker box if possible. Shut down all building reactors. Repeating: Terran forces are making groundfall..."

She slapped it and turned it off in the short distance she had that she could go straight before having to weave around more wreckage. She could see there was parts of fliers littering the road now, the crops on other side were smoking, and she could see at least two of the fliers had shattered glass globes and a tentacle with a half-crushed brain held in the graspers.

I'm not in here with you, you're in here with me! rang out in her memories, along with the hideous laughter the Terran had done as he had begun smashing at the stilter that had sucked out his brain.

Her long ears trembled with fear as she saw that there was a road ahead. So far she had had bad luck on roads. She slowed the car down, the engine whining, and came to a stop. She looked both way, saw nothing but darkness, and tried to figure out which way to go. The dirt road had been windy and twisty and she had no idea which way anything was now.

Left? Right? Just go straight? Ahead the road was narrow, like the one she was on, and vanished into the whufflegrain field. She squinted right. There was light on the horizon. She started to crank the wheel and stopped.

Light didn't mean anything good. Light could be the Terrans fighting the Slorpys or it could be a field on fire, or it could be a town being bombed.

She cranked the wheel left and slowly rolled out onto the larger dirt road. She wished she could see where she was going, where the road led, or where she was going. All she could do was keep driving and hope for the best.

Dambree had rarely left the little suburb she had lived in, going to city with her father once or twice a week didn't count, since he drove and she usually just paid attention to her dataslate. Now he life, and the life of her three younger siblings, *literally* depended on her figuring out where she was and getting them to a safe place and she had no clue where she was.

The car was starting to beep, steady tones, and a red light was flashing on the shattered display panel. Whatever it was, it was important, but with the display cracked and warped she couldn't tell what the problem actually was.

She turned a corner, going slow, and slammed on the brakes.

Bright streaks were coming from the sky. She could hear the rumbling and threw the car in reverse, backing up, as the streaks got brighter.

The first one hit behind her and her little sister screamed. Dambree threw it in forward and stomped the pedal, spraying dirt from beneath the tires as more impacts slammed against the road behind her, started hitting the fields around her.

She knew she couldn't go backwards, the only way was forward.

An impact hit the road directly behind her, lifting the back end of the electric car up slightly.

Her siblings screamed. Her little sister popped up from behind the seat, wrapping her arms around her neck as more impacts the road in front of her, exploding plumes of fire, smoke, and dirt into the air.

"Watch out!" her sister screamed.

"I KNOW!" Dambree screamed back.

Her little brother jumped over the back seat and into the front bench seat, his eyes wide. He grabbed the baby off the floor, who was screaming in anger at being woken up.

More impacts hit around them and Dambree was almost thrown out the door when a large piece of debris smashed into the ground and whirled off into the grain just a split second before she hit the smoking crater. The car whirred angrily as it cleared the far side of the crater and got airborne, then the springs squealed as the car hit the ground.

"Look out!" her brother yelled, pointing with one hand at the burning holes in the ground.

"I KNOW!" Dambree yelled back, yanking the wheel and narrowly avoiding a chunk of burning metal the size of the car. A tentacle writhed, segmented black metal, the graspers clacking on air even as she ran it over.

"Look!" her sister yelled, pointing into the field.

Dozens of streaks of light were whipping through the air, red and green and amber and purple, from dozens of points in the field. She could faintly hear tearing sounds coming from the field. Above the field were dozens of fliers that were rolling, trying to avoid the streaks of light and failing, trying to block them all with their tentacles and failing.

Do not approach Terran forces engaged in combat, she remembered.

The fliers were exploding. Every time they shined lights down in the field shafts of light reached back up from the field, causing explosions on the fliers surface that quickly tore it apart.

Dambree whined low in her throat and pressed the pedal harder, as if trying to push it through the floorboard would make the car go faster.

She managed to hit the brakes, warned by some sense that seemed to be getting more sensitive, just in time as shapes burst out of the grain. She screamed, throwing the car into reverse, as the shapes bounded out of the grain, across the road, and into the grain on the other side.

They were all black, quadruped robots with bucket-shaped heads. They had guns on their backs and were firing missiles from above their rear legs.

Dambree got that feeling again and slammed the car back into forward, speeding toward where the quadruped robots had crossed and vanished.

More quadruped robots, these ones less blocky, thinner and longer than the first group, more guns on the back, streaming across the road in a fluid group rather than just bounding across.

"Look out for the robots!" her little sister, Truba'an, called out.

"I know!" Dambree yelled back.

One of the fliers spun into the road, two of the sleek looking robots holding tentacles in their robotic jaws and firing the weapons on their backs into the underside of the flier. One braced its feet and Dambree saw, as she whipped the car around them, the ground dent inwards and blue energy flare at the robot's feet. The flier slammed into the ground again and the other sleek robot jumped on it, tearing with huge claws and tearing with heavy jaws full of fangs and sharp conical teeth.

Then they were past and Dambree held on the pedal.

"Why are they doing this?" Truba'an cried out, still holding tight around Dambree's neck.

"I don't know," Dambree coughed, pulling her sister's arms free. "Get in the front seat with your brother and stay down."

Her brother, Elurta, nodded, sliding down with the baby and hiding in the foot well. Her sister moved next to him, hugging him. All three of their faces were tight with fear, their triangular noses and whiskers twitching with fear, their ears pressed to the back of their heads, their mouths closed as they gritted their flat teeth.

She went around a corner, the edge of the car slipping into the grain, which lashed at her through the missing door, and saw steady lights in front of her.

CHARGE AND CARRY the sign said, blinking slowly. The price was blinking as Dambree pressed on the pedal as hard as she could, the little car thumping and bumping over the potholes and the bumps in the road.

It was in a gap in the grain, two other roads connecting to it that vanished into the grain, only one of the paved and glimmering with the induction fields for electric cars. The sign was still on, the interior of the shop lit up, and the charging stations sitting bright and shiny.

She pulled in slowly, coming to a slow stop next to the pump. She reached out and picked up the heavy Terran pistol, feeling the grip shift slightly in her hand as if to mold itself to her fingers.

"Can I have some nibbles?" Truba'an asked.

"Not yet. Let me look inside," Dambree said.

"There might be bad machines inside," her brother Elurta warned.

"I know," she said softly. She got out and moved to the back of the car, grabbing one of the quikcharge plugs as she passed it. She looked around and saw nothing but waving grain, although off in the distance several of the areas of lights from fliers sweeping the grain and streaks of light coming up from the ground in return.

The pump checked the cars onboard chip, not noticing it was cloned, and began pushing power through the cable an into the cars depleted batteries as Dambree ran up and ducked down next to one of the big cryplas windows. She peeked up and saw nothing, not even a shop-bot, then ducked down again. She counted to five, looking down at the pistol in her hand.

She wished she knew how to shoot beyond what she had seen on TV.

Push it against the temple, came up unbidden in her mind. She nodded and looked up again scanning. The rows looked clear, she could kind of see the coolers, and the counter looked empty. She stood up and rushed the door, her bare feet slapping on the plascrete. She busted through, her shoulder flaring with pain and making her cry out, but she was through and into the interior.

The little sensor went 'bing-bong' as she stumbled through the door.

She hurried, looking around the Carry-Out Shop, finding nothing and nobody inside. She checked the aisles twice, wondering where the teller or the shop-bot had gone to. Finally she moved back out and waved to her siblings to come in.

"Can I have some nibbles?" her little sister asked again.

"Yes, Tru, you can," Dambree said. "Both of you can pick up nibbles and sippers. Give me Pulnee."

Her little brother handed her the baby, who squirmed and tried to bite. Dambree pinched her nose to help her learn to curb her biting instinct as she headed over to the rack she had seen.

There. Disposable infant swaddling, artificial milk, a sucky, some stuffies, and an infant shirt that said "I <3 C&C" on it. She grabbed at it, carrying it back, batting her sister away from trying to grab one of her exposed nipples. She set the baby down, pulled the tab on the milky, and shook it. She felt it warm up in her hand as the nipple popped free. She handed it to the baby, who grabbed it with her two hands and stuck the nipple in her mouth before lifting her feet and putting them on the milky-bottle.

She quickly changed her sister's diaper, throwing the dirty one in the garbage.

"Tru, you watch Punee," Dambree said.

"You don't have a shirt on. Momma's gonna be mad," Tru said, a candy-bar in each hand.

"I know," Dambree said. She began moving stuff over to the back seat and the trunk of the car, hurrying as fast as she could. The car hadn't finished quikcharging and Dambree wondered if Alkree ever kept it fully charged.

The reminder of her boyfriend made her start to snuffle as she kept moving boxes of milky, nibbles, sippers, diapers, and anything else that caught her eyes. She packed the trunk then started putting it in the back seat.

She was behind the counter when she heard it.

The horrible sound of a floater.

"Here! Come here!" she snapped. She was glad that her siblings didn't argue, just ran around the counter and joined her. She slapped a sucky in Punee's mouth.

"Stay quiet," she hissed.

The floater was circling the store slowly. She could hear it making a weird fluttering, spluttering noise as it moved. She looked down at the pistol, seeing the light was red. She pushed it and it went green. The grip seemed suddenly more alive somehow and the pistol felt warmer even it did suddenly feel heavier.

The flitter moved around past the car. She peeked at it and saw it was damaged. Two of the tentacles were hanging down, sparking and trembling, the grasping ends missing. Two of the crysteel globes were damaged, shattered, the thick armor was divoted and cratered, missing in two spots and showing complex machinery and tubes inside. Several of the glass tubes were broken, sparks jumping from the base. It kept tipping on one side and having to fire its rockets to level out again.

It turned, the searchlight sweeping the inside and she ducked back down.

It moved in, Dambree could hear it, and there was a sudden crackling noise. Lightning played around the roof, arcs of electricity flowing to outside, and there was a high-pitched squealing noise. She could hear the rockets sputter as it pushed its way into the suddenly dark convenience store, the lights exploding in showers of sparks.

Her sister whimpered.

Grids of red light suddenly appeared on the walls, sweeping slowly across, and she knew that it was searching for her. The grid just like the cost-stamp detector in the stores.

Just like the grid that had passed over Alkree before the stilter had sucked his brain out.

There was a quiet hiss of liquid as her little brother wet himself when the grid passed over the counter, shining on the wall.

The sputtering got louder as the flitter roared forward, grabbing the counter with its tentacles and throwing it to the side.

All three screamed, turning around and throwing themselves against the wall, kicking their feet as their backs pressed against the cheap paint. The flitter reared back, as if it was startled, bringing its tentacles up in a defensive movement, knocking the shelves behind it down.

Then it started moving forward, several tentacles with intact graspers on the end sliding out of the body. It moved forward slowly, clicking the graspers.

YOU BELONG TO ME it whispered.

"EAT A DICK!" Dambree screamed.

It flinched back slightly, holding its tentacles up, then rocked back level, orienting to stare at her with wide lenses. There was a sense of glee as it started moving forward.

Dambree curled over her little sister, looking at her other two siblings. "Close your eyes," she whispered.

They both did.

Glass shattered at the front of the store and Dambree looked up in time to see something crash through the window. Its back was as high as Dambree's armpit, it had four legs ending in huge razor sharp claws, it had a tail, a long narrow head with huge heavy jaws full of spiked teeth, including tusks.

"SIMBA IS HERE!" the newcomer roared.

SIMBA AND MEWMEW

*"I've always liked robots, I like this robot most
of all."* – Old Iron Feathers

The big robot hurtled into the store, sliding, tearing up tile and plascrete with its claws as it slid to a stop in front of Dambree and her siblings. Two big tubes attached to belts popped up out of its back and a hazy curtain of dim light appeared in front of it. The flier jerked back, raising its tentacles, the feeling of malevolent glee vanishing and turning into something that tasted bitter, like ash, on Dambree's tongue.

The massive robot roared, opening its jaws and vomiting out greenish fire. The two tubes on the back roared, brass casings flying free, as solid shafts of light connected the new robot to the flier. The flier began jerking, explosions across the front. The lenses and the spotlights shattered, the tentacles blew free, and the flier blew backwards as fire gouted out of the top.

"SIMBA IS HERE!" the new robot repeated over the roar of BRRRRRRRT!

The flier hit its thrusters and jetted straight up through the roof, sputtering as it took off into the darkness, heading away from the convenience store. Dambree and her siblings screamed as cheap plas ceiling panels fell around them.

A port opened up on the back left leg and a tube dropped out. The big four legged robot gave a roar of triumph and bounded away, disappearing through the glass and into the night.

The tube made an odd noise. Almost like 'mew' to Dambree's shocked ears. She turned from staring out at the night and looked at the tube in time to see it grow a head and four legs, a tail popping up. It was like the big black one, only smaller and made of shiny metal like durachrome. Little whiskers popped out near its nose as it moved over to Dambree, who pulled her feet back at the touch of the little robot's whiskers.

Her siblings were crying, holding their ears, as the little shiny robot moved next to them and began rubbing itself against their ankles as it moved back and forth, rubbing against them all. After a moment Tru giggled.

"It tickles," she laughed. She picked up the candybar and began chewing on it.

Dambree watched as the little robot moved up to her legs and began licking the scrapes and scratches, leaving behind what looked like shiny saliva. The scratches hurt for a second, then tickled and went numb.

'mew mew mew' the little robot said. It gave itself a shake and seemed to grow fur, looking like a munskra, a little furry pet that many of the wealthier Hesstlin had. It moved into Tru's lap and began making a rumbling noise.

That was fine. Dambree wasn't afraid of it anymore. She'd always liked robots, and she'd just been saved by a big robot that had left the little one behind.

Dambree got up slowly, looking around for what she was after.

The shelf with the dataslates had been knocked over, most of the dataslates shattered when they had hit the floor. She found one that still had power and turned it on, tucking it into the waistband of her modesty wrap as she looked around again. She found the shirt-printer but the power was gone, the screen shattered, and the liquid plas leaking out of the side to form a puddle on the floor that was sticky as she nudged it with a toe.

"SIMBA IS HERE!" echoed through the night. Repeated from several other directions.

"We need to get moving," Dambree told her siblings.

"Can I take the mewmew?" Tru asked.

Dambree smiled and nodded. She liked the mewmew. She'd always liked little robots and she liked the mewmew most of all. "Sure. Grab some nibbles, a sippy, and lets go," Dambree told them. She came over and picked up Punee, moving back to the car.

Her siblings followed her, Tru holding the mewmew, which was loose in her arms like it wasn't solid, forming a U on her arms, the front and back legs nearly dragging on the ground as it continued to rumble.

Dambree tucked Punee back into her wadded shirt, which smelled like baby mess, popping the tab on another milky and waiting for it to warm up. When it was warm she gave it to Punee and made sure the baby was curled up on her side, sucking on the bottle. Tru and Elu got in, sitting on the floorboards, munching on their nibbles. The mewmew curled up with Punee, still making the rumbling noise.

Dambree unhooked the charging cable, ignored the flashing of "PLEASE PAY INSIDE", got in the car, and turned it on. She looked around, wondering where they were.

After a moment she realized it didn't matter where they were, they just had to go somewhere. In the fields the way she had came and to the right there were fliers sweeping the grain fields with searchlights only to be hit with streaks of lights that Dambree knew now were guns from the backs of those fast and aggressive robots.

She put it in forward and pulled out onto the dirt road, driving slowly through the darkness. Lights were still streaking down from the sky. Sometimes the object exploded, making more light falling, sometimes the light stopped and Dambree wondered if the object had vanished or stopped burning, other times the object got much brighter before dropping below the horizon or the level of the grain.

The car was still moving, the engine still whining, and she reached out and grabbed a bottle from the case she had put next to her.

She knew her mother and father wouldn't have approved as she popped the top open and took a long drink.

The carbonated alcohol drink was cool and fizzy as she gulped down half the bottle.

The dirt road wound through the grain fields, the only

sound was distant explosions, the rumbling of the mewmew, and eventually soft snoring from her siblings.

When she was sure they were all asleep she pulled off in a wide spot, leaving the car idling as she got out. She threw the empty bottle of fizzbrew into the grain, sat on the front of the car, put her face in her hands, and cried.

She felt the furry body of the mewmew wind around her ankles and sat down in the dirt. She felt stupid. Out in the dark, in a car that used to belong to a boyfriend who got his brains sucked out by a giant robot, no shirt, no brassiere, no pants, no shoes, no wallet.

No parents.

She startrf petting the rumbling mewmew as it rubbed itself against her shins.

The dataslate she'd pushed into the waistband of her panties made a pinging noise. Curious, she slid it out and looked at it. It shouldn't have been unlocked or activated since she hadn't run it through the register, but the screen was on.

A triangular head, with triangle ears, big eyes, and whiskers, all made of code, looked at her.

mewmew appeared on the slate at the same time as the mewmew made the noise she had named it after.

She looked down. "Are you doing that?"

A pinging happy tune pulled her attention back to the dataslate. The mewmew head had sparkles and ribbons spray from behind it on the screen of the dataslate.

PATIENT ONE: FEMALE HESSTLIN, 14 YEARS OF AGE, MINOR LACERATIONS AND CONTUSIONS, SEVERE CONTUSION (RIGHT SHOULDER), DAMAGED CARTILAGE (RIGHT SHOULDER), BLOOD ALCOHOL LEVEL 0.017%

PATIENT TWO: FEMALE HESSTLIN, 9 YEARS OF AGE, MINOR LACERATIONS AND CONTUSIONS, MINOR SCALP SWELLING

PATIENT THREE: MALE HESSTLIN, 11 YEARS OF AGE, MINOR LACERATIONS AND CONTUSIONS

PATIENT FOUR: FEMALE HESSTLIN, 7 MONTHS OF AGE, INTESTINAL GAS AND MINOR DIAPER RASH, RUNNY NOSE FROM

**POLLEN INHALATION, THREE TEETH EXITING GUMLINE
END MEDICAL REPORT**

She blinked at the information, then looked at the mew-mew again, tapping the screen. "You did this? You're... a doctor?"

The mewmew on the screen had a nurse's hat fall from off-screen onto its head and a thermometer appear in its mouth.

"A.. a nurse?" Dambree asked.

The mewmew on the dataslate had a green checkmark appear in each eye.

"I don't know what to do," Dambree said, hoping the little robot had an idea.

A picture of a flier and a stilter appeared on the slate with a small cartoon car driving away really fast.

"Run away? That's your suggestion?" Dambree said, shaking her head. "Well, I guess I'm getting that right."

The mewmew head reappeared on the dataslate, the eyes replaced with cartoon beating hearts.

The streaks of light and fire were raining down on the fields again, some of them brightening up. Some of them were shooting at each other.

An aircraft went by really low, low enough that the thruster-wash ruffled her fur. She could see the Terran Space Force logo of an armored hand crushing a planet on the wings. It was followed by a half dozen, all of them moving so fast that she barely heard them before they went by.

The dataslate had an image of the car driving, leaving behind a cloud of dust.

"You're probably right, mewmew," Dambree said. She picked up the mewmew and went back to the car, setting the mewmew down then getting in right afterwards. She sighed, picking up the heavy pistol and putting it in her lap before putting the car in forward and pressing on the pedal.

She began driving through the darkness, any intersections taking the ones that led her away from the falling lights and the burning grain. She could see the red from where the grain fields were catching on fire, where the fighting was still going.

The road suddenly intersected with a paved road with the induction coils and she stared at the black plascrete for a long time. Cars were going by, slowly moving to the right and left, each of them fleeing toward where the others had fled. Some cars had baggage on top of them, some had broken windows. She could see car windows with children's faces pressed against them. See where some doors had been torn off. In the middle median people were walking, two lines, each walking the other direction. She could see people crying, see kids holding onto parents, see children walking alone.

Dambree had no idea what lay in either direction.

Across the street were more fields.

She moved the car out, ignoring the people slamming on their brakes and honking their horns, moving slowly across the first lane and into the shoulder. People turned to stare as she moved up the median and waited.

The line paused and she moved slowly through it.

"Everyone looks so hopeless, mewmew," she said softly.

The crowd screamed as another pair of aircraft whipped by, their noseguns hammering, back the way Dambree had come from. Some people ran into traffic. Horns honked and cars swerved, one car hitting several of the people walking. People began screaming as another flight of aircraft screamed by overhead, several of them firing off missiles that went hypersonic within meters, the loud ka-RACK echoing through the night.

The missiles hit fliers that had been sneaking through the darkness, illuminating them. Four exploded, but there was over a score more. They all hit their searchlights, the wide lenses glittering, all of them with at least one blue globe, their tentacles snaking out and graspers snapping.

The crowd and the drivers panicked.

Dambree was almost through the crowd when a car swerved, plowing into the crowd, slamming into the back passenger side of the car, spinning it slightly. She looked over to see a screaming male Hesstlin pinned between her car and the front of the other car.

Someone grabbed at her, trying to yank her out. She looked over and saw a male, grabbing her arm with one hand and the steering wheel with the other. His eyes were wild, panicked.

"JUST GIVE ME THE CAR, YOU LITTLE BITCH!" he screamed.

The first of the fliers had reached the highway, tentacles ripping people out of the windows, out of the tops of the cars. Some rushed forward on stuttering thrusters, reaching out and grabbing the fleeing members of the screaming crowd.

"No! GET OFF!" Dambree said, pulling back at the waist.

"GET OUT!" the male screamed, yanking her hard. Something popped in her elbow and fiery pain went up her arm. Other people in the crowd were reaching into the car, trying to grab at her, grabbing at her supplies in the back, trying to grab the steering wheel. All she could see were howling mouths, wide eyes, and grasping hands.

Dambree grabbed the pistol, holding it out at the male grabbing onto her, who was being joined by two more, even more coming up behind them.

"You don't have the..." the male started to sneer, reaching for the pistol.

Dambree pressed the firing stud.

The pistol gave a loud WHAK!, the recoil hurting her wrist, the mag-coils at the end of the barrel flaring with orange light for a second.

She didn't notice any of that.

The man's upper body exploded into scraps of flesh that sprayed the people behind him. One arm sailed into the air, trailing blood, the other arm spun away. The male behind him that was reaching for Dambree went down with his entire chest blown out.

The mewmew jumped up and fired little sparkling fireworks that poured red smoke from them out of its mouth, out through the window, and into the crowd. People started coughing, moving back from the smoke, but others didn't care and rushed into it.

She swept the pistol around, firing twice in front of her at the people rocking the front of her car, even as she stomped on the accelerator. The round grazed a female trying to pry the hood up, tearing off her arm. The other one took the mag-ac round to the stomach and was blown in half, blood and gore showering around him. The round kept going, killing people behind them, injuring others.

The car lurched forward, bumping over people in the way. One screamed and went under the front, but Dambree didn't care. She managed to get the car across the street and into the grain field, bounding into the ruts, leaving the crowd and the highway behind.

She was crying again, the pistol in her lap, her arm dangling by her side, driving with one hand. Her forearm and hand tingled numbly and her elbow felt like it was broken. She couldn't believe she had done that. Her mind kept replaying the way the one holding onto her had exploded into shreds.

The mewmew climbed up on her lap and nuzzled her arm. After a moment it went numb around the elbow, the fiery pain going away. A few moments later she felt its little legs wrap tight around her biceps and then around her forearm. She slowed the car and looked down just in time to see the mewmew somehow lengthen.

Her elbow gave a loud *pop* and feeling came back.

The mewmew jumped back on her lap.

She started crying as she slowly moved through the field, the grain rattling and whipping the bottom of the car.

It wasn't fair. Why did the Slorpys have to attack? Why did they have to kill her boyfriend, her parents, all those people? Why couldn't they have just left her and her people alone?

She was snuffling as the sun slowly rose.

She was getting more and more tired. The stimfizzes weren't helping, even though she chugged two. Her limbs were heavy with exhaustion, her eyes felt gritty, and her ears were drooping.

The sun had just cleared the horizon when the car suddenly left the grain and slowly whirred onto a carefully manicured lawn.

In front of her was a two-story house, big and sprawling. Farm machinery was scattered around, there was clothing gently waving in the breeze, hung from suspended lines. The house was painted blue with white edges.

She could see the holes in the roof and the broken windows from the Slorpys.

This should be safe. They've already been here, she thought to herself, carefully steering the car around to the front.

"Stay here," she told her siblings, who responded by snoring.

She got out of the car slowly, picking up the pistol, which felt much heavier in her hand, and walked toward the door.

She wasn't sure if she was hoping there was grownups in it or not.

So far, my luck hasn't been too good, she thought to herself as she walked up the porch, trying to be quiet.

She pulled open the screen door, bracing it with one bare foot, then turned the handle on the door. It opened up, revealing a dark and shadowed front room. She moved inside the house.

The doors slowly swung shut behind her and closed.

THE FARMHOUSE

The inside of the house was cold, the lights off, only the Tri-Vee flickering in one corner, showing a female Hesstlin, dressed in professional clothing, silently speaking. She looked exhausted, the chiron below her was scrolling by addresses, datalink hyperlinks, com-numbers, and warnings not to approach ongoing fighting.

Dambree glanced at it and dismissed it. She'd lost her datapad and now was just carrying a hacked one she'd stolen from a charging and convenience store. She padded through the front room, looking around carefully. The front room was empty, the dining room was quiet, but the windows were broken. She went around the table and saw the body of a male Hesstlin, not much older than her, the top of his head gone and the interior of his skull thick with flying insects.

She turned away, gagging, to stare at the table, breathing heavy and trying to keep herself from vomiting. She focused on the table, with the knocked over chairs around it. There were dishes with cold food, a few insects crawling on it, on the table, with a knocked over glass of juice. She moved to the kitchen and found leftovers still on the stove and the dishwasher was open. By the broken open back door was a female Hesstlin that was her age, half out the door, with a pool of dried blood around the flattened top of her head.

Dambree turned away, opening the fridge door, trying not to think about how easily it could have been her.

The fridge door squeaked when she opened it. There was food and bottles of alcohol.

She grabbed one and opened it, taking a long drink off of it.

It was sharp, bitter, and soothed her aching throat.

She moved back into the front room and slowly up the stairs, the bottle in one hand and the heavy pistol in the other. She still couldn't believe she had shot that man, more, she couldn't believe the way he'd just exploded into chunks. Dambree glanced down at the pistol and saw the light was burning green. The digital display on the side, that she hadn't noticed before, had several numbers on it and the letters LOW-V APERS on it. She had no idea what it meant and went back to paying attention to slowly moving up the stairs.

At the top she found an adult male Hesstlin. He had a power rifle in his hands, but it hadn't helped and the top of his head was missing. Dambree carefully stepped over him, for some reason afraid of touching the dead man.

She opened each door, peeking in.

Her brain edited out the crib in one room where the window was broken next to it.

She started to close the door on one room, then opened it back up. There were posters on the walls that she recognized, all new stuff from the time Terrans had arrived. The same kind of music she liked.

Dambree moved into the room quietly, looking around.

It felt wrong. Like she was stealing as she opened the dresser drawers. She started pulling out clothing, heavier than the light and soft stuff she usually wore. The dead girl's chest wasn't the same so Dambree settled for just a shirt. Then a pair of pants, good heavy tough cloth. Dambree usually wore comfortable shoes that didn't need socks, but she took a pair of socks anyway and slowly rolled them onto her feet and up over her hocks. In one of the pictures the dead girl, who still had a brain in the pictures, was wearing a checkered shirt on top of the shirt, the front unbuttoned. Dambree looked around, found a brown and gray one, and put it on, rolling up the sleeves slightly.

Looking in the mirror she felt stupid.

The girl's feet were smaller than Dambree's, so she checked the other room and found that one of the pair of boots worn by the boy her age fit. Part of her wanted to wear the soft shoes he had, but instead, remembering the last night, chose the heavy boots with the dirt on them.

She found the adult female in the bathroom, half pulled through a hole in the wall.

Sighing, she got blankets off the beds and moved through the house, covering the dead with the blankets, trying to be as quiet as possible.

Once that was done she went back out to the car. She woke up her siblings, the baby only biting her twice, and brought them inside, Mister Mewmew following them. She moved her sister and brother over the couch, where they gratefully sat down then laid on their sides. She changed the baby's swaddling then fed her, holding her and using the slow rocking back and forth to help ease her own anxiety.

Dambree wanted to tell Mewmew to stay out from under the sheets and blankets, but was just too tired. Mewmew would move under the sheet, be under there for a few minutes, then come back out.

She realized she had dozed off when she heard the roar of aircraft going by overhead. First the sputtering thrusters of the fliers, then the roar of Terran aircraft's engines and the thunder of their guns.

Dambree sat up and looked around. The sun was high and the grain was quietly waving outside. The car was sitting near the front porch, covered in dust, and her siblings were still asleep.

She ached, her elbow, wrist, and shoulder ached and when she cried out in pain moving her arm Mewmew moved over and started rubbing against her.

The pain in her arms eased.

She stood up and yawned, then picked up the bottle of beer, taking a long drink off of it and looking around.

When she remembered that her mother would disapprove of her drinking alcohol she remembered what had happened to her mother. She went out on the front porch, sat on the steps, and quietly cried. Mewmew curled up next to her, purring, as she cried for her twice killed mother.

Dambree hoped her father was dead, not powering some Slorpy robot. She closed her eyes and wished real hard that the Terran soldiers had killed the robot that had sucked out her father's brain.

The dataslate in her pocket pinged and she slowly pulled it out.

Another medical update. Minor exhaustion had been added as well as severe anxiety. Mewmew recommended more sleep.

"Thank you, Mewmew," she said, petting the robot, which made it produce that low rumble.

She yawned and went back in, laying back down with her siblings, and closed her eyes.

"Bree, wake up. Bree," Tru said, shaking her, her voice pitched low.

Dambree woke up with a jerk, the pleasant dream of sitting in class with nothing exciting happening dissolving.

"hwa?" Dambree slurred, then wiped her eyes and mouth. "What?"

"Shh," Tru said. She was crouching and pointed outside to where the sunshine had paled and rain was drifting down. "There's things out there."

"What?" Dambree asked, picking the pistol up off the floor.

She grabbed the bottle and took a drink off of it to ease her sore throat.

"They look like big bugs. Like, up to my knee," Tru whispered. She looked around, "Mewmew went out to see them and I think they did something to him."

"Why?" Dambree got down on her hands and knees, wincing at the pain and stiffness in her joints, and started crawling to the broken from window.

"There's like two of the big black bugs just standing there, they have lights flashing over their heads," Tru said. She peeked up. "See, over by the car. They were doing stuff to the car."

Dambree looked over the windowsill. The rain was coming down hard, the clouds low and heavy. She stared at them for a second, having never seen purple clouds before. The lightning in the clouds was green and orange, flickered up in the clouds, not coming down to earth. She could see flares of light in the clouds that for some reason she doubted were lightning.

Dambree looked at the car and frowned. The hood over the engine was raised up and the engine shroud had been flipped up.

"Behind the car a little bit," Tru whispered.

Dambree could see Mewmew. The little robot was still, in between what looked like foot tall insects that had four legs, regular arms with little hands, and pointy arms. The insects were all in black and she squinted at them. It didn't look right and it took her a moment to realize the insects were wearing black armor and carrying tiny rifles and tubes the size of her finger.

"See, there's some in the car," Tru whispered.

Dambree looked back at the car in time to see two climb out of the engine, one of them pulling a wire with it. The two insects quickly attached the wire, tugging on it to make sure it was affixed correctly.

"What are they doing?" Tru asked.

"I'm not sure," Dambree admitted.

Mewmew suddenly turned around, trotting back to the house. The insects scurried away, off to the side, and Dambree wondered where they were going. The mewmew jumped in through the window, saw that Dambree and Tru weren't on the couch, and reoriented. When it saw them it made noises that sounded like "murr-row" and "me-ow" as it moved over.

Dambree's dataslate pinged and she pulled it out of her pocket. The picture on the dataslate was of the mewmew and the big bugs all dancing and waving pompoms with cartoon hearts for eyes.

"You know them?" Dambree asked.

The picture changed to the mewmew and the insects standing under a waving flag with the armored hand crushing a planet of the Terran Space Force.

"You're both Space Force? What do the bugs do?" Dambree asked. Tru kept pushing against her, trying to see the dataslate.

The picture changed to show a cartoon car looking all sad. One of the insects, green and more delicate looking than the ones she had seen, scurried up holding a wrench. The insect flashed a happy face icon over its head, tapped the car with the wrench, and the car suddenly was gleaming and new looking and looked happy. The insect scurried away.

"They fix things? Cars and stuff?" Dambree asked.

The cartoon mewmew reappeared and sparkles shot out around it.

"Should we..." Dambree started to saw.

Mewmew hissed, turning to face the window. On the dataslate there was a pictures of Dambree, Tru, Elu, Punee, and the mewmew moving low across the floor on their fingers and toes to hide.

"Let's go," Dambree said. She hurried over to the couch, grabbing Elu, who woke up with a startled outcry but shut his mouth when Tru hushed him. She scooped up Punee, who was asleep still, and hurried upstairs.

She led them past the room with the empty crib.

"Hide in the closet," Dambree ordered. Another shock was that her siblings didn't argue, just took Punee and hid in the closet, giving her a bottle of milky that Dambree had pulled the tab on. Dambree laid down by the bed, setting the dataslate next to her, holding the pistol with both hands.

She could hear the sounds of fliers, the thrusters stuttering. She had gotten a peek out of the window and seen stilters out in the grain, slowly approaching. She peeked over the bed and gasped.

There was dozens, maybe even hundreds, of stilters slowly moving toward the house, through the grain. Most of them had all of their globes lit up blue, very few of them looked damaged. There were fliers moving in with them, most of their globes were blue too. There were other ones too, smaller, with only a single globe, that floated along on a single sputtering thruster.

put it right against the temple, she thought to herself, looking down at the pistol in her hand.

Hesstlin started exiting the grain, staggering, many of them weeping, trying to run but at the ragged edge of exhaustion.

There's no kids, Dambree realized.

The dataslate beeped and Dambree looked down at it. It showed a cartoon version of everyone getting in the car and driving away in a cloud of dust.

"Come on, we've gotta go," Dambree said, standing up. The crowd was a third of the way across the huge back yard, getting close to the tractors.

Which suddenly started, raising whirling blades and clattering cutters.

The people coming out of the grain field shrank back with a cry of dismay that Dambree could hear even though she was busy picking up Punee and trying to not get bit. She didn't have time to flick the baby's nose to teach her not to bite, but instead just tucked Punee under her armpit like a purse and hurried toward the stares.

There was a small sounding 'brrrrrrrrrrrrrrrt' outside, along with sharp whistling noises followed by cracks.

Whatever was going on, Dambree didn't know. She just knew she had to get to the car before the crowd did. Had to get her siblings in the car and get far away from the Slorpys and the crowd both.

They thundered down the stairs, not bothering with being sneaky, and ran for the car. A big bug had just shut the hood when it raised the tube, aiming it above Dambree's head. The tube belched fire and a streak went over Dambree's head.

Something behind her blew up as she whipped open the door and slid in, getting behind the steering wheel. She set the baby on the floor as her little brother and sister got in and Mewmew jumped onto the floor boards.

The car started up as Tru pulled the door shut.

The insect, Dambree could see the Space Force logo on its back now, cocked the tube and leveled it again. Dambree looked over and saw one of the single-globe things, much smaller, level out and extend out two thinner tentacles.

The insect jumped off the hood, scurrying to side, and firing the tube again. Others must have been hiding in the grass, because at least four more rockets hit the little flier, sending it spinning and crashing to the ground. Before it could move two of the black insects jumped on it, slashing at it with blades that looked like they were made of solid energy.

Dambree missed it, having pressed the accelerator to the floor. The electric engine caught and slammed Dambree against the seat as the tires bit and the car leaped forward. A female Hesstlin came around the corner of the house and bounced off the front fender as Dambree went to turn, lost traction, then overcorrected before overcorrecting again.

"WATCH OUT!" Tru yelled as the car slid around the side of the house and shot forward.

The wrong way.

"I KNOW!" Dambree yelled back as the car sped *toward* the stilters and fliers and the crowd.

One of the farm machines had somehow acquired heavy guns that were firing at the fliers, yellow-ish orange fire erupting from the fliers.

"THE CROWD!" Elu shouted.

"I KNOW!" Dambree yelled back, turning the wheel. She turned too sharp and the car went sideways, sliding toward the crowd. It got close enough that two people reached out, tried to grab Dambree. One missed, the other grabbed on and was dragged for several feet before they suddenly vanished and the car bumped over something.

"THE TRACTOR!" Elu yelled as Dambree swerved wildly, fishtailing in the grass.

"I KNOW!"

The huge tractor had the spinning blades up, guns on the roof of the cab and on the fenders firing at the Slorpys. As they shot by Dambree saw two of the insects wave from inside the cab.

Tru waved back.

The car, seemingly able to go a *lot* faster, sped by the house and Dambree was more careful with the turn, even then the car went sideways until Dambree got it back under control and sped down the dirt road. No longer raising a small cloud and barely keeping ahead of it, but going so fast it made Dambree's eyes tear up. The rain flew in the cab, soaking her and her siblings.

"Bree, here," Elu said. When Dambree glanced over he was holding out a pair of sun blockers.

"Thanks," Dambree said, putting them on her face, over her eyes. It dimmed the day a little, but now the rain and wind wasn't hitting her in the eyes. "Hand me a bottle."

"Mamma wouldn't... oh..." Tru said as Elu handed over a bottle.

"Eat a nibble and drink a sippy," Dambree said, letting go of the wheel long enough to pop open the bottle. She took a long drink then put the bottle between her legs. She checked and breathed a sigh of relief when she felt the pistol still next to her.

Her siblings didn't argue, just dug into the supplies, coming back with sweet nibbles and sippies.

"Where are we going?" Elu asked.

"I don't know. Where the Slorpys aren't," Dambree answered.

"The fighting scares me," Tru said.

"I know," Dambree said.

"Mommy and Daddy aren't coming back," Elu said softly.

"I know," Dambree said, slowing down so she could weave around a large flier that was broken into at least three pieces.

"Are we going to die too?" Tru asked. Dambree glanced over as she took another drink of the fizzybrew and saw her sister was crying.

"We're going to try not to," Dambree said.

The four children and the purrboi raced down the road, outrunning their own dust and the battle.

THE CABIN BY SPARKLING LAKE

"Fear not the evil man, for you know he will do. Fear the good man who's back is against the wall and his loved ones behind him, for he will do anything he must." – Treana'ad proverb

For all she knew, she was driving in circles. Every time she was forced to choose which way to go the only way that mattered was away from smoke, white lines in the sky, or the sound of explosions, lightning, and buzzing. The car ran smoother and she was grateful for that. Her brother and sister played with the dataslate, playing games with Mewmew, while the baby laid on the floor in front of the passenger side of the bench seat and gnawed on her sucky to help her new teeth come in, the whole time glaring at Dambree with her amber eyes.

She drove with a bottle between her legs and the pistol on her lap, keeping one eye on the charge level, which was working again. She had no idea that the car was getting a lot better milage out of the charge that previously, the quick tuneup altering the mechanisms to be far more efficient.

Every time she finished a bottle, she slung it out the door, leaving it on the dirt of the road. At crossroads she slowed down and dropped a sippy bottle out the door to mark that she had gone that way prior.

The dirt roads were a long winding maze between fields of grain, fruit, and vegetables. The rain stopped and the day got hotter even though there was still heavy cloud cover.

She came around and corner and slammed on the brakes, making her siblings cry out and Mewmew stand up with its rear paws on the seat and its front paws on the dash.

In front of her was a black metal thing, stretching across the road, disappearing into the grain on either side. It had holes in it that no longer smoked, although she could see sparks inside of it. It had dozens of thick insect legs and she could barely see thick treads on the other side of the insect legs. It had protrusions, bulges, and half open irises.

She backed up quickly, driving almost a mile in reverse before she found a large enough spot to turn around. At the intersection she made sure to mark that one with three sippy-bottles before taking a left and hoping for the best.

An hour later she realized that she had only one way to go, and that was toward more smoke. She sighed, checked the pistol, seeing again LOW-V APERS on the little tiny display on the side, and set it in her lap. Her elbow hurt on her left arm, her wrist and shoulder hurt on her right arm.

She never thought driving could be tiring but Dambree felt like someone had stomped on her shoulder blades and back, her legs ached, and her feet hurt.

Driving toward the smoke, watching the sun slowly lower, she saw one of the big towers and slowed down. It was tall, at least two hundred feet tall, a metal lattice reaching up in the sky with dishes on the top and blinking lights.

"We're hungry," Tru said.

"I know. Eat a nibble," Dambree said.

"We're tired of nibbles," Elu said.

"I know. So am I," she said, taking another long drink off the bottle and slinging it out into the grain.

"Punee's stinky," Tru informed her.

"I know," Dambree said. The baby had been stinky for a while, but so far had seemed content to sit there with a full diaper and gnaw on her sucky.

The tower turned out to be in the middle of an open spot and Dambree pulled over, next to the tower, and shut off the car.

"Let's have something to eat, go potty, and walk around," Dambree said, getting out and stretching. She almost dropped the pistol but caught it.

"There's nowhere to go potty," Elu whined.

"Pee on the back tire of the car. Nobody will watch," Dambree said.

Elu looked a little huffy but went around the back of the car.

"Mewmew is watching," Elu complained.

"Mewmew's a robot. I'm sure you'll be fine," Dambree said, picking up Punee, who promptly tried to smack her. Dambree grabbed a swaddling and another milky. She popped the tab on the milky, waited for the nipple to pop up once it was warm, then handed the milky to Punee, who spit the sucky out and started sucking on the milky.

At least she only tried to kick Dambree twice while she was being cleaned and changed. Dambree picked up the sucky, put it in her mouth to clean in, then put it in her pocket.

"Are those your clothes?" Tru asked. "They don't look like your clothes."

"I know. They are now," Dambree said. She walked to the back of the car, pulled down her pants, and squatted, leaning against the back bumper.

"I have to pee too," Tru said.

"Go ahead," Dambree said, sighing in relief. Tru pulled her nightgown up and followed her sister's example, staring off at the field of grain like her sister.

"There's no potty wipes," Tru said.

"I know. Sometimes there isn't," Dambree said, standing up and pulling her pants up. She buckled the belt and shook her head, looking down at herself. A fuzzy checkered shirt over a dark shirt, heavy pants, boots.

She wouldn't have been caught dead wearing those clothing a week ago.

"Let's have a picnic next to the car," Dambree said, digging in the back. She found some can of self-heat and started holding them out until her siblings each grabbed a can. She found a nice soup, picked Punee up, and walked over to where her siblings were sitting on the plascrete base of the tower.

"It's going to be dark again soon," Tru said.

"I know," Dambree said, staring at the fields.

"Mewmew's climbing the tower," Elu said.

"Mewmew will be fine," Dambree said, shoveling the food into her mouth. She didn't notice that it didn't really have a taste to her. It was almost mechanical, shovel the thick soup into her mouth, chew, swallow, repeat.

"Can we go..." Tru started to say when Dambree heard a faint roaring noise, getting louder.

"Get in the car," Dambree ordered, grabbing Punee up, who promptly passed gas and laughed.

"But Mewmew," Elu started.

"Mewmew can take care of himself," Dambree snapped, hustling to the car. She climbed in, waving at her siblings, and laid down, holding all three of them tight.

The roaring got louder. It sounded like the Slorpys but not sputtery. It circled once then got really loud before cutting off. There was a whining sound overlaid by heavy sounding footsteps coming up to the car.

Dambree looked up and screamed.

It was a jet black bipedal robot with a skull face, wings lowered to the sides of its body, and a big gun with a drum underneath it. It looked fearsome and Dambree knew right there that her long run had come to an end.

She yanked out the pistol and put it against her brother's temple.

"Weapon lockout," the armor said.

The pistol beeped and the words vanished to be replaced by "LOCKOUT" on the side.

"Vat Grown Luke, kid, you were about fucking snuff your brother for no reason," the big black robot said.

Dambree looked back at the robot in time to see the skull split down the middle then pull back to each side, revealing a brown skinned primate like the one she had hit in the middle of the road. The primate was sweaty, with eyes that had a glow in them that was slowly fading from red to amber.

"A Terran!" Tru squealed, wiggling to get loose.

Dambree sat up and Punee bit her arm, gnawing on it and drooling.

"What are you doing out here? This whole region's a battle-field," the Terran said, moving up and kneeling down.

"Running," Dambree said.

"Bree shot some people! They were trying to grab our stuff and one grabbed Punee and tried to pull her out of the car, but Bree shot them! She didn't have a shirt then! Bree ran over some people! Bree stole clothing! Bree stole the nibbles and sippies!" the words all came tumbling out of her siblings' mouths.

The Terran just nodded, looking serious. "That sounds like you've had an exciting night," the Terran said.

Mewmew vaulted through the window and into Tru's lap. Tru started petting her without thinking about it.

"Bree didn't pay for the stuff we got from the store or for charging the car," Elu said. "There were bugs fixing the car but then they started shooting at Slorpys so Dambree drove away!"

"Bree ran over a Terran then a Slorpy got him then the light turned red on the Slorpys head and it started hitting itself," Tru snitched.

"That where you got the pistol, kid?" The Terran asked.

Dumbree just nodded.

"That's a dangerous weapon," the Terran said.

"I know," Dambree said, thinking about how the guy trying to pull her out of the car had exploded.

"I'm going to unlock it if you promise not to shoot your lit-tle brother," the Terran said.

Dambree nodded and the pistol beeped. When she looked at it it read "Hi-V DP" on it. It flickered for a second and settled again on "Lo-V APERS" like it had showed before.

"All right, this whole region is a shit-show and you can't stay here," the Terran said.

"Why not?" Tru asked.

The Terran looked at her then pointed at the tower. "That's

a wireless signal repeater. Right now those are priority. You got lucky I heard your purrboi's SOS signal."

"Where do we go?" Dambree asked.

The Terran heaved a breath in and out. "I'm trying to raise an Evac Hospital or a Refugee Point, but the commo net is all hash," he(?) said. "You can't go back into the cities, and out here is dangerous."

"I know," Dambree said.

"To be honest, every time we put up an evac or refugee point those Precursors mass assault it. They really want large groups," the Terran said.

"They suck out people's brains. SLUUUUURP!" Elu said.

"Yeah, we figured that out earlier today, kid," the Terran said. "These aren't like the other ones, these ones are a lot different."

"Oh," Dambree said. "Have you seen machines like that before?"

The Terran shook his head, a quiet whirring sound accompanying it. "No, these ones suck out brains."

"I know," Dambree said softly.

The Terran lifted up one wrist and Dambree noticed that his arm was thicker than her thigh. His wrist had little pointed cones slightly sticking out at the back of his hand. A panel opened up and a hologram appeared.

"OK, you're here. The bulk of the fighting is over here. Some of those Telkan Marines are over there, you don't want to go there. This spot the clankers have air superiority for now," he mused, tapping at the map. "It's still touch and go over here. That's a major clanker Ell-Zee there. Hmmm."

To Dambree it just looked a mottled green and brown mess with squiggles, weird shapes, and red or yellow crosshatched areas.

He shut it off. "All right. Does your car's GPS work?" the Terran asked.

"GPS?" Dambree asked.

"It's autonav," the Terran said.

"Uh, no. I broke it last night," Dambree admitted.

"BREE STOLE A CAR!" Tru crowed out.

Dambree sighed and hung her head with sudden guilt. She'd robbed and murdered her way across the entire night.

"Hey, kid?" The Terran said gently.

Dambree looked up, tears shining in her eyes.

"Don't," the Terran said. He reached out and lightly patted Dambree's left shoulder. "Don't do that. I can see the clankers tried to get into your car a couple of times. You made it through the night."

"A man was grabbing on me, trying to pull me out of the car. I shot him," Dambree admitted.

The Terran nodded. "Yes, you did. And you and your siblings are alive."

"The other Terran said not to let them take us alive," Dambree admitted.

"No, you don't want to do that," the Terran agreed. He unhooked something from his belt and tossed it to her. "See that ring?"

She looked at and saw there was a metal ring at the top with a lever down the side. "Yes."

"You pull that ring, open your hand so the lever pops off, and by the count of three it will blow up. It'll be quicker than trying to do it with a mag-ac pistol," the Terran said. "It's a M81A6 high explosive with white phosphorous jacket enhanced fragmentation grenade with a phasic pulse. If the clankers want you after that goes off, they better bring a sponge."

Dambree nodded slowly, getting the gist of it.

"Trust me, kid, don't let them take you alive," the Terran said.

"I know," Dambree said. "They took our father and mother," she said softly.

"I'm sorry," the Terran said, and strangely, seemed to mean it.

"What's a 'Simba', Mister Robot?" Tru asked.

The Terran turned to Tru. "It's a feline cyborg. Big,

heavy duty combat chassis, packs dual 20mm three-barrel ro- tating autocannons, 30mm plasma ejector, mortar and missile launchers, battlescreens, and carry a four-pack of purrbois. Why?"

"That's where we got Mister Mewmew," Tru said, holding up Mewmew, who was dangling from her arms like he didn't have bones.

"Ah. I wondered where you got that. Keep Mister Mewmew close, kiddo," the Terran said. He suddenly looked up then back at Dambree. "You have a datapad?"

Dambree held out the datapad to the Terran, who put his finger against the input port. The dataslate started flashing then stopped, showing a map.

"There, I uploaded a possible route. Right now, get out of here, this whole place is on the edge of going atom smasher," the Terran said. "I put directions to a nearby forest. Head there, fol- low the directions," the Terran crouched slightly and the wings snapped out. "There's some cabins up there and a camp-site store. Rob the store, go to the cabin I marked. Stay there."

Dambree noticed the Terran's eyes were beginning to glow red.

The face shield closed and again Dambree was staring at a black skull.

"When do we come back?" Dambree asked.

"Someone will come get you. Stay quiet, stay alive, kid," the Terran said. He suddenly jumped straight up. Dambree saw him jump at least fifty feet in the air, then with a roar the engines on the back fired up and the human flew away.

"He left," Tru said softly.

"I know," Dambree said. She looked over and saw that Tru and Elu both were crying. "We have each other, we'll be all right."

She looked around, saw the only thing they were leaving behind were the empty self-heat cans, and started the car. It shuddered for a moment then the engine leveled out. She put it in drive and pulled out, noticing the dataslate reoriented. She handed it to Elu.

"Here, you watch that. Tell me if I need to turn," Dambree

told her little brother.

"How come he gets the dataslate?" Tru asked.

"Because I need you to take care of Punee. He's a boy, she'll bite him," Dambree said. "You can hold Mister Mewmew too."

"Oh," Tru said. She shifted Mister Mewmew and looked down at Punee, who was holding onto the milky-sippy with her hands and feet as she gnawed on the nipple. "She looks OK right now."

"Good," Dambree said, steering around the wreckage of a pair of fliers.

She followed the directions that Elu kept giving her, only having to turn around twice when Elu miscalled the directions. The sun was slowly setting behind the clouds. She cracked open another fizzybrew and took a long drink off of it.

Several times massive shell casings rained from the sky, other times shards of armor, and once a flier fell from the sky and slammed into the road in front of her but she managed to swerve around it. Once a Terran vehicle crashed out of the grain, huge, all black, with a massive barrel on the front and clattering tracks instead of wheels. It had vanished into the tall grain before she could even scream, the yell of "OUT OF THE WAY, JACKSASS!" floating through the air after it.

It slowly got dark and Dambree found out that one of the headlights had been fixed, giving her an OK view of the road. Tru and Elu went to sleep, staying asleep even when Dambree pulled over to squat next to the car and pee then change Punee's swaddling. Eventually the trees began to slide by on either side of the road, getting thicker and thicker, until she was driving through a forest, on a dirt road, in the dark, with only a single headlight to guide her way.

She kept the pistol on her lap even as she kept drinking the fizzybrews and slinging the empty bottle out of the car through the empty door frame.

It was nearly midnight when the dataslate beeped and she glanced at it, seeing she needed to turn. She slowed down, keeping an eye out, until she saw it.

The dirt road had a sign next to it that made Dambree wonder if the Terran was right.

DANGEROUS BRIDGE

She closed her eyes, sighed, and took a deep breath. The bridge couldn't be more dangerous. She turned onto the dirt road and headed slowly up. The bridge was wood and clattered as she crossed it. She could see the stream below and wondered how deep it was.

Dambree almost drove past it. The sign wasn't lit, the windows were dark. It read 'PackGuru's Camping Store' and the door was shut.

Rob the store, went through her head and she wondered if Terrans often broke the law.

She braked and got out, making sure the Punee was asleep. She was frowning, her fists balled up, chewing on her sucky. Mister Mewmew looked up from where he was curled up on Tru's lap, who was leaning against her brother and drooling.

"I'll be right back," Dambree said quietly.

A logo appeared on Mister Mewmew's face. :-)

Dambree turned and headed to the store.

She would walk all the way around it before going in.

Dambree's recent lessons had taught her to be cautious.

She peeked in each window, seeing nothing but darkness. Each door she tested was locked. She went and got a big rock and used it to smash in the plexglass window, reach in and fumble around till she found the lock, then unlock the door.

She took her time, moving slowly, partly from exhaustion and partly to be careful. A flashlight first, which she kept on dim. Then camping gear, more food, a water filter, and whatever else caught her eye. There was a small portable "Dr. Fusion" generator that she managed to cram into the back seat on top of the sleeping bags and plas wrapped pillows.

She also took two emergency hand-crank radios and a pair of night vision eye-wraps, which let her turn off the flash.

Once the car was as full with as much she could cram inside of it, she locked all the doors and got back in the car. Mister Mewmew flashed her another :-) as she followed the twisty road. She passed by several dark cabins and wondered why the Terran had chosen one so far away.

The cabin was at the end of the dirt road, with cliffs on three sides of it. There was red streaks in the dark rock, trees overhung the cabin, and the lake was only a little ways away.

Dambree parked the car and stared at it.

It looked like nobody had been there since the Overseers had fled.

Why here? she wondered. She looked at the cliff walls. *The rock looks like its bleeding.*

Still, she explored the cabin, this time with Mister Mewmew following along. It had a kitchen, two bedrooms, a front room, and a fireplace.

No power. The stove took wood.

At least there was an axe on the wall next to the door.

She woke up Elu and Tru to help her and together they unloaded the car. Dambree didn't get mad at her two younger sibling's whining. She was just as tired as they were.

"We have to get it all in case it starts raining again. Some of the food got ruined when the rain soaked through the paper," Dambree said.

Finally, it was done. Dambree tucked them both into their sleeping bags in front of the fireplace and kissed their forehead. Punee didn't even try to bite her, just glared at her with her amber eyes.

Dambree dragged a chair next to the fireplace, so she could see the window and the doors, put the ball with the ring and lever on the table next to her, and stared out at the darkness.

She kept the pistol in her lap even while she eventually slept.

Dambree woke up with a jerk, reaching out for her mother, half standing up. The pistol fell to the floor with a dull thump, making Mister Mewmew open his eyes and look at her for a moment before closing his eyes again. Dambree sat back down, bent forward, and picked up the pistol before looking out the windows.

The sun was up, sunlight streaming through the trees to make patterns of light and shadow on the forest floor. The car was dirty, dusty, the roof ripped in three spots, the fenders dented, the windshield and back window gone, and missing the driver's side door. For a moment Dambree almost panicked at the sight of the empty seats and the open trunk, then remembered she had moved it all inside with Tru and Elu's help.

Dambree stood up, put the pistol in her waistband, and stretched. Her knee and hock popped loudly as she stretched up as far as she could. Her shoulder hurt, making her wince when she tried to raise her arm, and her elbow hurt on the other arm. She wandered back to the back of the cabin, where the kitchen was, and picked up a can of self-heat and a bottle of fizzybrew before she went back and sat down.

Outside she could hear small animals moving around and the noise of birds, once in a while broken up by the faint roar of aircraft going by in the distance, but nothing like the world-consuming roars of when the aircraft had passed by overhead while she was driving.

When she was done eating she put the can in the garbage, used the outhouse, cringing at the pottywipe that had spiderweb and bugs on the surface, and wandered around the cabin.

She found a firepit with old bottles and cans in it. A small pile of garbage hidden and half-devoured by a bush, a shack full of chopped wood with a smaller axe hanging on the door, and a bra hanging from a bush branch that was faded and rotted out. She found a handle on a pipe coming out of the ground and moved it up and down a few times. On the fifth try rusted water poured out and she went back to moving the lever, feeling resistance now when she pressed down and pulled up, until the water was clear and clean.

Several times she heard aircraft roar by in the distance and every now and then she'd hear the faint sounds of an explosion. The sky still had streaks in it as falling stars whipped across the sky.

I hope you're not the Slorpys, she thought to herself as she saw a large group of streaks falling from the sky, heading east.

She sighed and went back inside, finishing the fizzybrew and dropping the bottle into the garbage. She grabbed another one and opened it, the bottle auto-chilling when the cap was released, and took a long drink off of it as she quietly prowled around the cabin.

It was neglected. Cobwebs, dust, a few leaves in the corners, but it wasn't that bad.

It was better than being out on the road and having to stay moving.

She found a hatch in the wooden floor and, grabbing the ring and pulling, opened it up, wincing at the squeal of dry hinges. A ladder dropped down with steep narrow steps. She grabbed the eyecovering and went down inside, the light enhancement brightening the basement to daylight. It was largely empty, just a pile of chopped wood in a corner, empty shelves, and an old rodent nest long abandoned.

Seek shelter in basements, she remembered.

Dambree moved extra sleeping bags and several cases of self-heats, some packages of milkys, a few boxes of sippies, and some swaddling downstairs, putting them on shelves.

Just in case.

Her siblings were still asleep. Punee frowning and making fists, Elu sprawled out like a roadkill squirrel, and Tru curled up in a ball inside her sleeping bag.

Part of Dambree wished she could go back to sleep, but she knew what was waiting if she did.

Memories.

Grabbing another bottle she headed back outside, sitting on the stump between the battered car and the cabin. She set the extra bottle down and took another long drink.

Staying here till someone comes and finds us won't be too bad, she thought to herself. *I doubt anyone's posting to GalNet right now. Nobody probably cares about selfies or quick little comments on Zimmer, nobody cares about statuses or relationships or whatever.*

For a second the thought went through her mind that her mom and dad would have to upgrade their status to "brain bot" and "dead" and she started laughing quietly, sobbing at the same time, rocking back and forth for a moment.

She inhaled deeply and stopped herself from crying and laughing. She took another long drink off the crisp bitter fizzy-brew and flicked her long ears a few times to calm herself.

Another set of aircraft went by, these ones close enough and fast enough they made the trees sway slightly. By the time she'd glanced up they were gone. She realized she had learned the difference between Slorpy and Terran aircraft engines. Slorpy sounded sputtery, Terran ones were a steady roar.

Part of her wished she could go back.

But she knew, there was no going back. Not now.

The leaves crunched behind her and she turned around and looked.

Elu and Tru were coming up behind her, Tru carrying Punee, who was glaring at everyone with her beautiful amber eyes while she gnawed on her fist and drooled.

"How long do we have to stay here, Bree?" Elu asked quietly.

Aircraft roared by overhead and in the distance were rapid-fire explosions that echoed off the cliff.

"Till we don't hear that any more," Dambree said.

"Oh," Tru said. She sniffled and moved around next to Dambree, setting Punee on the ground on her stomach. "I miss mommy."

"I know," Dambree said. Punee was pulling her knees up to her stomach and kicking, trying to move forward.

"I miss mommy and daddy," Elu said. He started sniffling.

Tru began to wail, crying loudly, tears running from her eyes.

There was bright white flash that made everything seem flat, then a faint rumble that she could feel through her shoes.

Tru and Elu began crying harder.

Dambree jumped to her feet, grabbing both of them by their ears. They each grabbed the arm holding their ears with both hands as she lifted them slighty.

"DON'T CRY!" she bellowed. She shook them by her ears, even though she had always told herself she'd never do that to her kids like her parents had done it to her. She yanked them close, off balance. "Don't cry! Hold it back! Let it turn to something else. Just let it turn - to something else!"

She let go of her sibling's ears.

"Don't cry. Not for momma, not for daddy," Dambree told them firmly. She picked up the dropped bottle of fizzybrew and took a long drink. "Babies cry, we aren't babies any more."

Punee had rolled onto her back and was glaring at her. Dambree moved over and rolled Punee back on her stomach.

There was another flash followed by a rumble through the ground a few moments later.

"You see that? You hear that?" she snapped at her siblings.

They both nodded.

"That's the Terrans and the Slorpys killing each other. They aren't even our people and the Terrans are trying to stop the Slorpy's from killing us and stealing our brains because we can't. You saw all the dead Terrans on the roads. You saw that Terran die. He didn't cry, did he?" She said.

They both shook their heads.

"The Slorpys killed him and he didn't cry about it," Dambree said, staring at the woods, which had gone silent. "Don't ever cry again."

Both nodded slowly and even though Dambree could see the doubt inside of them she didn't say anything. Mister Mewmew curled around her legs, purring, them moved to Tru's legs.

"Let's get something to eat then we'll do chores," Dambree said.

"I don't wanna do chores," Elu said.

"That Terran didn't want to die, but what you want and what you get are two different things," Dambree answered.

They were silent as she picked up Punee and carried her inside, only having to flick her nose twice to stop her from trying to bite. Elu and Tru ate their self-heats silently, sucking at the straws on the sippys as they stared at her.

"We're going to dust, then sweep, then wipe everything down," Dambree said. "There's two bedrooms. I'll take one, with Punee, you two get the other."

"I don't want to sleep with a boy," Tru said, crossing her arms.

"People in Hell want water. Both of you are shit out of luck," Dambree quoted her Terran gym teacher. She sighed. "We'll put up a curtain."

"Where do we take a bath?" Elu asked, twitching his ears as he looked around.

Dambree sighed and looked around. There were big plasteel tubs hanging on the wall next to the stove and she cocked her head, her ears twitching as she thought. "In those tubs. We'll use the pump outside to fill buckets of water, warm them on the stove, and take a bath in the tub."

"But Elu might see me naked," Tru protested.

Dambree turned and looked at her. "We'll hang up curtains or something."

"Just because you drove around without a shirt so all the boys could see you naked doesn't mean I want Elu to..." Tru started to say.

Dambree slapped her and Tru stared in shock, her mouth hanging open.

"I drove around in my panties because if we stopped for me to get clothes, you would be dead," she hissed at her sister, leaning forward. "You don't get to judge me for what I did to keep you three alive. Not now, not ever, do you understand me?"

Tru nodded quickly, her head bobbing up and down and her ears flat against the back of her head in a sign of submission.

Dambree glared at her sister. "I *killed people* to keep them from hurting you. I *shot* them. I ran them *over*. To keep them from hurting you."

"I'm sorry," Tru said quietly.

"I know," Dambree said, turning away. "I am too, Tru."

"I love you," Elu said quietly.

"I know. I love you too. You and Tru and Punee. I love you all very much," Dambree said. She moved over to the sink and looked at it. There was a pump handle next to the faucet and she started moving it. It took six tries before she got any resistance and the first gush of water was dark brown with rust.

It was silent, except Punee fussing while she tried to scoot forward.

"Let's take a break. Have a sippy and a sweetie," Dambree said, setting down the damp rag she'd torn from a rotting curtain.

Tru and Elu moved over and opened the cupboard where they'd put the food away. Tru chose frosting covered cookies and Elu chose cake nibbles. Both came down and sat down next to Dambree as she popped the top of a fizzybrew and felt the bottle chill in her hand.

"Do you love me?" Tru asked hesitantly. "You don't hate me, do you?"

Dambree shook her head. "No, I don't hate you, Tru. I love you more than you'd ever believe right now."

"I love you too," Tru said, and leaned against her.

When Dambree put her arm around her little sister it seemed to make everything right.

Aircraft roared by overhead. A lot of them, close enough to the ground that it rattled the windows.

"We're going to be here a long time, aren't we?" Elu said in the silence afterwards.

"If we're lucky," Dambree said.

"What about Uncle Inkree or Aunt Fenn? Can we go stay with them?" Tru asked.

Dambree shook her head. "No, we'd have to go back to where they're fighting. We're lucky we got away."

"They're probably dead or hiding like we are, stupid," Elu said.

Dambree smacked her brother across the back of the head. "Don't call your sister stupid."

"I'm sorry," Elu said.

Tru just nodded. She didn't know why, but Dambree looked

different. Like she'd lost weight but gotten bigger somehow. Tru didn't understand it and she didn't understand why it made her want to hold Dambree and cry.

But she wouldn't cry.

Dambree didn't know what was going through her sister's mind as she got up and got the broom to sweep the floor. She was thinking about how she'd need to hang up stuff to keep light from being seen from outside, how she'd need to figure out how to start a fire in the stove, how she'd have to haul in water from the pump to fill the bath.

When she was done sweeping, she picked up Punee, who had gotten little stinky, and changed her swaddling, noticing that Punee needed a bath. Mister Mewmew jumped up on the table and nuzzle Punee, who tried to grab him, then backed up. He bumped Dambree's hand until she looked down.

"What?" Dambree asked, wondering what the strange little robot wanted.

The dataslate pinged and Dambree shifted it so she could see it. An animated hand showed up, then an animated Mister Mewmew head. The Mister Mewmew puked up some paste looking stuff and it showed the hand rubbing the paste on Punee's privates and the rash going away and the cartoon Punee smiling.

"Um, all right," Dambree held out her hand. Mister Mewmew made some horking sounds and barfed up thick white paste. Dambree smeared it on Punee, flicking her on the nose once. After a moment Punee relaxed slightly and Dambree reswaddled her.

"Thank you, Mister Mewmew," Dambree said.

Mister Mewmew showed a ":-)" on the smooth area on top of his head, then jumped down.

Dambree ran her finger inside of Punee's mouth, ignoring how Punee tried to clamp down. There was two little bumps and one little hard spot that felt like the tooth had broke the gum but was still stuck inside.

"You're gonna get teeth soon and we'll switch you to yummy paste. Yes we will," Dambree said.

Punee snapped at her, glaring, but Dambree didn't bother

to flick her nose.

"Give me a nibble, one of the hard cookies," Dambree said.

Elu brought it over to her. "Are you still mad?"

"No. I'm not mad at any of you," Dambree said honestly. She took the cookie and gave it to Punee, who immediately went to gnawing on it. When aircraft roared by overhead Punee glared at Dambree as if it was all her big sister's fault.

It was getting dim outside and Dambree set Punee on the floor on her stomach to get exercise and moved to the window.

Dark, ugly clouds had gathered. Lighting flickered in the clouds, but not lightning like Dambree had ever seen. It was purple, orange, and green. Thick bolts with lots of tracers that snarled among the clouds.

Dambree took a drink off her fizzybrew and stared outside.

"Can me and Tru play with the slate?" Elu asked.

"Play some games with Mister Mewmew," Dambree said, taking another drink.

It started to rain. It took her a moment to realize what was so strange about it.

Everything was slowly gaining a dark stain, like it was shadowed. Mister Mewmew ran outside then back inside, showing ":-(" on his head.

"Mister Mewmew, I don't understand," Tru said.

Dambree moved over and looked at the slate. It showed cartoon versions of everyone going downstairs into a hole and smiling then switched to everyone sitting upstairs and starting to look sick. Dambree looked out at the rain, which was coating everything in black that looked sticky.

She moved over and pulled up the hatch. "Everyone inside. Now."

"But it's dark," Tru said.

"Take a flash," Dambree said. "Elu, get a box of food and some sippys."

Elu nodded.

"Tru, get some milky and some swaddle," she said. She bent down and picked up Punee. "We're gonna hide downstairs for a little while."

"Are the Slorpys coming?" Elu asked, his voice tight with fear.

"I don't know. Maybe," Dambree said. She grabbed the sleeping bags and tossed them down the hole, kicking the pillows after.

"How long do we have to stay down here?" Tru asked, carefully stepping down the ladder steps.

"Until Mister Mewmew says it's safe," Dambree said.

She closed the hatch over her as she went into the basement.

Outside, the rain kept coming down, coating everything in black as the heavy clouds, born of atomic detonations, relieved themselves of the heavy particles and dust they'd been filled with from the uptake.

Off in the distance another atomic hammer smashed. Then another.

The brutal fighting for Hesstla continued, the only options victory or death.

Either was fine.

TASK FORCE TIAMAT

Ground fighting intense. Regrouping at 32% and rising. 92nd Infantry and 51st Infantry are securing population centers. 1st Cav and Second Telkan are still engaged with the enemy. Hotel Company, Dinachrome Brigade is still engaged in heavy action. Situation is still extremely chaotic. Civilian refugee camps are priority targets for Precursor forces.

The fight for the high orbitals is still ongoing. System control is still in flux. Precursors do not flee at 10% casualties as well as show advanced fleet tactics.

Precursor vessels used psychic weaponry as well as psionically assisted weaponry.

At this time, all SUDS are still redlined.

Further situation report to follow.

---NOTHING FOLLOWS---

BUGS, BABIES, & BAD MEN

"Because they can." – Pubvian saying regarding
the strong and the weak.

"Look," Tru said, pointing at where Punee was laying belly down on the floor. The little infant had pushed herself up on all fours, her little elbows wobbling as she gave a big nearly toothless grin, her sole tooth peeking out of the gum glistening with drool. She was staring at her sucky, which sat where she had spit it, just beyond her reach.

"I see her. Good girl, Punee. Good girl," Dambree said, smiling at her sister, who was starting to rock back and forth, primal instincts trying to get her to move.

Punee's feet kicked and she fell chest down on the floor, her little pointed chin thumping against the floor of the cellar.

Dambree could hear her growl of frustration as Punee glared at the sucky as if it was the sucky's fault she'd fallen.

Punee kept kicking her feet, trying to get purchase, and scooted forward an inch or so.

"She's getting dirty," Tru said, unwrapping a nibble.

"She'll be fine," Dambree said, leaning back against the cool stone wall of the cellar and closing her eyes.

After a moment Elu spoke. "She's eating dirt off the floor."

"She'll be fine," Dambree said, not bothering to open her eyes.

"Ew, she ate a bug," Tru squealed.

"She'll be fine," Dambree said, sighing. She opened her eyes and stared at Punee, who was busy chewing away, slobber coating her fuzzy chin. "See, the bug came out the loser."

"She ate a bug," Tru protested.

"Yeah, well, it doesn't seem to bother her, does it?" Dambree sighed. She reached over and picked up a bottle of fizzybrew and popped the top, feeling the bottle cool in her hand.

"But she ate a bug," Elu added.

"I know," Dambree sighed.

"I'm bored," Tru whined.

"I know. Play a game on the slate with Mister Mewmew," Dambree said, then took a long drink off the bottle, soothing her sore throat. She'd had a nagging sore throat since her crazy flight from Makeout Point that refused to go away.

"I want to play too," Elu said.

"I know. Tru, play with your brother," Dambree said, closing her eyes again. Her ears were tilted back, pressed against the stone wall. Faintly, from a long distance, her sensitive ears felt a rumble through the rock.

They're still fighting up there. It's been two days, she thought to herself. *That's a good thing, I guess.*

She closed her eyes, sipping at the fizzybrew, as Tru and Elu played with Mister Mewmew on the dataslate. She's noticed that the majority of the games Mister Mewmew played with them had educational themes underpinning them but were still fun enough that her younger siblings wanted to play them over and over.

Every now and then Dambree would open one eye and check on Punee, who was busy pushing herself up on her hands and knees before rocking back and forth until she fell down. Every time she landed back on her tummy she'd growl in frustration and struggle to try again.

You'll get it, Dambree thought, watching for a moment.

She had cracked open the next one when Punee laid there for a little bit, her eyes closed, then relaxed, moving from awake to asleep without the little baby noticing it. Dambree saw that Punee was kicking slightly in her sleep.

Learning dreams, Dambree thought to herself. She remembered that tidbit from school, from Health Class, taught by a three foot tall russet mantis person.

She wondered what happened to Missus *Lessons Show the Way* when the Slorpys had invaded.

Miss Way *would probably just tell me to make sure that Punee doesn't bump her soft head on things and let her try and fail,* Dambree mused, taking another sip off the drink.

She suddenly realized that the insects that had repaired the car, had armed the big tractors, and who had fought the Slorpies from modified farm equipment, were probably related to Miss Way.

Dambree shook her head and sighed.

She felt Mister Mewmew butt against her foot and looked up. Her siblings were eating out of cans of self-heat and Mister Mewmew had pushed the dataslate to her. She picked up the dataslate, lifting her knees and resting it against her legs so she could see the slate and Mister Mewmew both.

"Yes?" She asked softly.

A picture of cartoon trees appeared with rain. It showed Mister Mewmew standing on his hind legs and checking the rain and air with a datapad. Mister Mewmew had on a lab-coat like a doctor and glasses. It looked kind of silly to Dambree and made her smile.

"You need to go outside?" she asked.

Mister Mewmew's picture shot sparkles and ribbons.

"I'll come with you," Dambree said, grabbing the dataslate and pushing herself up against the wall.

Mister Mewmew frowned as well as had a :-| appear on his forehead.

"You two stay down here, Mister Mewmew and I are going upstairs," Dambree said.

"Why?" Tru asked.

"To look at the rain."

"Why?" Elu asked.

"To see if the rain is still black," Dambree said.

"I don't like black rain," Tru said.

"I know. Neither do I," Dambree said. Mister Mewmew had

already gotten to the top of the stairs and was oozing through the wood hatch. Dambree tucked the dataslate into her belt, pulled down the last of the fizzybrew in the bottle and set the bottle in the cluster of empties, then followed.

When she opened the hatch the smell of wet forest rushed into her nose, making her sneeze three times in quick succession. The doors and windows were still closed and the interior of the cabin dry as she got out and slowly closed the hatch. The pistol was heavy in her waistband as she moved around slowly.

It was late in the day, the shadows deep in the woods around the cabin. As she watched Mister Mewmew oozed through the closed door.

The first time she'd seen that it had creeped her out, now it didn't bother her at all.

She set the dataslate on the counter and grabbed a can of fizzybrew, cracking it open and taking a drink. Dambree leaned against the counter, sipping at her drink, watching the rain fall. The black sticky stuff had been washed off and now the rain was clear, washing away the dust and dirt. The car looked better than it had since Dambree had ripped the door off, making her feel a little better.

After a bit, Mister Mewmew came back in, showing a smiley face on his head.

"Is it better now?" she asked.

The dataslate pinged and Dambree watched the cartoon that came up. It showed a bomb exploding into a fist-like cloud that had stink lines radiating off it. The stink lines went 'up' and hit clouds, which started emitting stink lines. Then rain fell, all of the oversized drops surrounded by stink lines. The rain fell on a car, trees, rocks, all of which began to emit stink lines. The cartoon then switched to a Terran looking at a strange looking instrument that made the stink lines glow. The Terran moved to a rocket, punched in numbers, and the rocket launched into the clouds, where it exploded in a puff of dust. The cartoon focused on the dust, making it larger and larger, until it reveal the dust was really super-tiny machines. It showed the machines looking around with big googly eyes for stink lines. When it found a stink-line it would wave to the others and they would rush up and cover the thing emitting the stink-lines. The little machines would take pieces out of the atoms and eat them and the stink lines would go away.

"Nanites? Terran nanites to get rid of radiation?" Dambree asked. She vaguely remembered learning about radiation in science class. It was why reactors were dangerous and why the Lanaktallan forbid them from being on the surface of the planet, instead using giant solar collectors in orbit and beaming the power down to massive receptor stations in order to provide power to the planet.

The cartoon Mister Mewmew appeared, its eyes replaced with beating cartoon hearts and sparkles and ribbons shooting off from behind his head.

"That's good to know," Dambree said. "Can they come up?"

The cartoon switched to Dambee and her siblings in the basement while the sun went twice across the sky before they climbed out with big smiles.

"Two days. OK. Two days, we can do that," Dambree sighed. She moved over to the hatch. "It could be worse."

The cartoon Mister Mewmew nodded, its face serious.

Two days passed slowly for Dambree, who watched Punee get better and better at moving around. She kept moving backwards, which made her growl in frustration. Dambree had learned quickly that as soon as Punee saw the pistol she'd try to get to it, but so far she could only scoot backwards, so she always ended up moving away from it.

Dambree managed to convince Mister Mewmew to put instructions for the pistol on the dataslate and while Punee and the others were sleeping she would do the firing stances for the pistol, learning how to use the holographic sight on the top, even how to use the 'non-firing training mode' to practice her aim. Dambree learned how to set the different ammunition types, marvelling that they all come from a solid block of metal.

Still, every time she set it down and Punee saw it, the baby would try to reach it, scootching backwards instead of forwards toward what she wanted.

That didn't stop her from trying, and when Dambree put it in her pocket she'd glare at Dambree with her beautiful amber eyes, baring the tiny sliver of tooth that had managed to extend past the gumline.

She also ate a couple of bugs.

Dambree just shrugged. It seemed to make her happy, so Dambree just figured the bugs were shit out of luck, as her gym teacher would say.

Tru and Elu had a big fight the second night over the last choco-nibble. Dambree solved it by taking it away and eating it herself, giving Punee half of it, ignoring her younger siblings' protest that it was the last one and both of their favorites.

Tru and Elu sulked till they went to sleep.

For a long time after her siblings were asleep, Punee chewing on her own fist and frowning while she kicked, Dambree stayed up and stared at the darkness. She could see Mister Mewmew open his eyes now and then to stare at her, but he usually went back to sleep.

Dambree sat in the dark, nursing her fizzybrews, staring at the shelves that were lost in the darkness.

Her mother and father were gone. She hoped that the Terrans had destroyed the Slorpy that had gotten her father so that her father was no longer inside of it.

She kept having nightmares of her father inside one of those crysteel globes, screaming as he was forced to hurt other people, pounding on the crysteel and tearfully begging to be let go. Every time she woke up crying and shivering.

Which is why she was nursing her fizzybrew when she heard it.

A vehicle. The whining of the electric engine.

She got up quietly, checking the pistol in her pocket. She snuck up the stairs, carefully opening the hatch and sliding out. She closed it and kicked the carpet over it, staying ducked down in the darkness.

A single door slammed and Dambree froze, listening closely, as she half-crawled to the couch and peeked over. After so long in the basement the night looked brightly lit to her.

There was an adult walking around the car, kicking the tires and looking inside. He was wearing eyeshades and had on a LawSec uniform.

Dambree opened her mouth to call out, feeling a flood of relief that a LawSec had found her.

Then the man turned around and Dambree closed her mouth.

The tan of the LawSec uniform was dark, had a tear in the front. The badge was flashing red instead of showing the LawSec officer's face and ID number. The man didn't have the belt that all LawSec wore.

There was something about him that made her mouth go dry and her little tail twitch.

The man walked up to the door, opening it. He walked inside and looked around, his glasses obviously letting him see in the dark.

"Lotta loot here," he mumbled. He took a step forward and stopped, staring at where Dambree was crouched down behind the couch. "Well, hello there, little miss," he said, his voice sounding friendly.

Dambree knew, she didn't know how, but she *knew* that it was faked.

"Hello," Dambree said, standing up and moving slowly to put the table between her and the strange man.

"Where are you parents, little girl?" the man asked, moving forward with her, a smile on his face.

"I'm here all alone," she lied.

"Are you now," the man said. He looked around. "You drive that car yourself?"

Dambree nodded. "Yes, but I wasn't good at it."

"You in town down the road when all the fighting started?" the man asked, slowly moving around the table.

Dambree moved with him, keeping the table between them. "Yes," she lied.

The man stopped, putting his hands on the table. "Well now, someone should protect you, little miss," he said. "There's killer robots around and the Terrans are killing everything that moves."

"They are? I thought they were our friends," Dambree said.

The man shook his head. "Nope. They're helping the robots kill everyone. I saw it with my own eyes," he said. "They kill any of us they find, just like the robots."

Dambree knew that was a lie. The Terrans could have killed her a dozen times and had done nothing but help when they could.

"Oh," Dambree said softly. She reached out and grabbed a bottle of fizzybrew, cracking it open and taking a sip.

The man copied her and took a can, taking a long swallow. When he was done he smacked his lips and looked at her, his eyes hidden by his dark glasses. "You shouldn't be drinking this stuff, little miss. You don't look old enough to be drinking."

Dambree didn't answer, just shifted around the table a little so she had her back to the back door and took a drink.

"You know, maybe I should stay here and protect you," the man said slowly.

"You'd protect me from the Terrans and the robots?" Dambree asked, trying to sound innocent.

"Well," the man said, and his smile got wide and ugly, his ears, shorter than Dambree's because he was a male, stood straight up from his head. "Maybe if you're nice to me I'll protect you."

Dambree swallowed thickly, getting a gut feeling what he meant. "Nice how, mister?" she asked, taking a sip and dropping her hand under the table.

The man's smile got uglier. "How about we start by you taking off those shirts?"

Dambree started shivering, covering what she was doing under the table with it. "My momma said never to take your shirt off in front of strangers," she said in her best little girl voice.

"Your momma isn't here, little miss," the man said. "If you're old enough to be drinking booze, you're old enough to be nice to me if you want my protection."

Dambree yanked her hand up toward the end of his sentence, her thumb over the top of the fizzybrew, and sprayed him in the face with the dark foaming liquid. Before she even saw the effect she turned and bolted, throwing her shoulder against the back door and crashing through.

She got about ten steps before his hand grabbed one of her ears, yanking her backwards. She gritted her teeth so she didn't scream as he pulled her around and back handed her, sending her sprawling to the ground. The pistol fell from her waistband and the man saw it.

"No you don't, little girl," he laughed, stepping forward and kicking it away. Dambree rolled on the ground, trying to get away, but he kicked her in the back.

Dambree grunted, unwilling to cry out, her hands going to her back.

The man stepped on one of her ears and looked down at her. He reached up and slowly removed the eyeshades.

Dambree went still, staring in shock.

His eyes were sunken in his head, bloodshot, the flesh around the eyes was missing the normal fur, the flesh bruised black, with dried blood on the fur beneath them.

"Take off your shirt," the man ordered.

Dambree nodded, reaching her hand up. The man licked his lips, leering, and put his eyeshades back on.

Before Dambree could get the first button undone the man yelled out in pain, jerking back from Dambree and looking around.

"Something bit me!" he cried out. He staggered to the side and Dambree noticed he was starting to drool. "Bit me! Bit my ankle!" he slurred out.

Dambree saw Mister Mewmew dart forward, his mouth open to reveal sharp little teeth and two long fangs, and bite the back of the man's other ankle before darting away. Mister Mew-mew didn't look soft and cuddly, instead he looked like he had a black shell that drank in the light.

The man staggered away, mumbling "biting me, bit me, bit my ankles" as Dambree slowly stood up. She walked over and picked up the pistol as the man crumpled to the ground. She lifted it up, then lowered it before putting it back in her waistband.

It would be loud and scare the little ones.

Mister Mewmew trotted up, rubbing against her ankles as she walked over to the shed. She opened the door and took down a tool hanging on the wall. She looked down when Mister Mew-mew made a noise. The unhappy face was on his head.

"I have to, Mister Mewmew," she said softly, standing in the rain, the tool in her hand.

She walked back to the man slowly. He was on his back, staring up at the sky. He was breathing heavy, panting, foam ooz-ing out of his nose.

"Help me, little girl. Help me," he said.

Dambree hit him in the face with the shovel until he didn't move any more.

Mister Mewmew followed her as she dragged the man back to his vehicle. It was a LawSec car and Dambree carefully went over it. She found nibbles in the glove box, supplies in the trunk after Mister Mewmew cracked the lock, including a big gun and a bunch of really fat bullets with plastic casings. There was a belt for a neural pistol in the trunk and she took it, hiding it under her checkered shirt, tossing the neural pistol onto the top shelf of the cupboard, and put the heavy pistol into the holster.

She carried everything into the cabin, setting it down. She took two breaks, drinking a fizzybrew each time, then when she was finished cracked open another bottle of fizzybrew and walked back out to the cars. She moved her little battered car she had inherited from her boyfriend to behind the cabin, then walked back to the LawSec vehicle.

She had dumped the man's body in the trunk.

Dambree opened the door to the LawSec vehicle and looked down at where Mister Mewmew was sitting on the ground, looking at her.

"I need you to stay here and guard the littles, Mister Mewmew," she said. Mister Mewmew showed a :-(on his head, but faded away. Some time while she had been working Mister Mewmew had gone back to looking fuzzy and soft.

Dambree got behind the wheel and started it up, turning around.

Dambree drove slow through the dark, until she saw a turn-off from the main road that led to other cabins, further away. She drove the car to next to one of the cabins and stopped, leaving the lights on and the car on. The battery was only at a third as she got out and turned on the spotlight to shine on the front of the empty cabin.

She dragged the man's body out of the trunk and over by the door, laying him on his back, facing up, and dropped his broken eyeshades on his face.

Dambree knew she couldn't leave the LawSec car in front of her cabin. It would attract too much attention.

Leaving all the lights on, knowing it would quickly drain the battery, she walked away, through the rain, and down the road.

She knew it should bother her. The man had still been alive when she had started to hit him with the shovel, not making any sounds but grunts of effort. It should bother her, knowing she had killed him.

It didn't. Not even the gurgling noises he had made or the wet meaty thwacks the shovel had made.

She took another drink off her bottle of fizzybrew.

Dambree knew it wouldn't have just been her. She didn't know how she knew, but she knew that when he found out that her siblings were in the basement he would have hurt them too, maybe even killed them.

Her ear still hurt from where he had grabbed it then stomped on it.

She finished her fizzybrew, slinging the bottle into the woods, and walked down the road. She didn't really think about anything, her brain in neutral as she just put one foot in front of the other. She was soaked through but didn't care, just walking through the darkness. Her ear and her shoulder hurt, and her butt hurt from where she'd hit the ground, but the pain receded as she walked through the rainy night.

After a little bit Dambree came out at the intersection. The store was in front of her and the long walk back to the cabin was to her left. She sighed, realized that she was thirsty again, and headed into the store.

She went in through the back door that she'd left unlocked. This time, after she got a fizzybrew, she looked for things she hadn't thought of before. She got a couple of boxes with games in them and stacked them up, then grabbed a large backpack with a metal frame so she could shove the boxes inside of them. She grabbed a few medical kits when she saw it.

CAMPING FOR NOOBZ was the title, and it showed a confused Terran staring at two sticks with a sad looking tent half collapsed behind him and a big furry animal running away with a wicker basket that had a red and white checkered cloth fluttering out from it.

She grabbed that, walking back and shoving it in the backpack.

Curious, she looked behind the bar, looking under the counter. She was surprised to see a bat under the bar, but she got it and went back to put it on the frame of the backpack. She added some camping tools to the frame, and a sleeping bag at the bottom, then attached a waterproof cover to it.

Picking up the backpack, she went back and stood behind the bar, looking at the handles, licking her lips. After a moment she set the backpack on the bar, picked up a glass mug from the shelf, put it under the nozzle, and hit the lever.

It blew spluttery foam into the mug. She held it down until fizzybrew started pouring out.

It took her a couple of tries to get a mug full that wasn't

mostly foam. By the time she managed it the first one had settled, the foam gone, and the mug half full. She picked up the mug and took a long drink, closing her eyes.

Which meant she heard the vehicle pull up.

You have to be kidding me, she thought, bringing down the mug. She heard two doors slam as she refilled the mug, watching the front door.

Two men came into the bar. They looked around and when they saw her setting the fizzybrew mug on the bar they both smiled.

"Hey, now, little miss," one said.

Dambree slid the mug down the bar, happy it only spilled a little bit. It came to a stop at the end and both of the males watched the mug.

She started filling another one.

"This your bar?" they asked.

"My daddy's," she lied. She finished pouring the fizzybrew into the mug and slid it down. "He got slorped."

Both men moved up and picked up the mug as Dambree reached down and picked up another mug. They drained their mugs quickly, but Dambree filled up two more, sliding them down the bar.

"Say, you ain't seen a friend of ours, have you?" one asked. He was portly and heavy-set, jowls on either side of his mouth. Dambree could see a slight discoloration in his fur below his eye-shades.

"LawSec?" Dambree asked, feigning disinterest, pretending she was one of the rich and popular girls at school, or a Lanaktal-lan.

"Yup, that's him, little miss," the fat one said.

"You're a cutey. He say anything to you?" the other said, setting down his almost empty second mug. Dambree smiled at him, noticing that he too was wearing eyeshades and there was a slight discoloration below his eyeshades.

"Just that he wanted me to be nice to him," Dambree said. She pointed at the mugs in front of them in the dimness. "Another?"

"Yeah, pour us a couple more, little girl," the first one laughed.

"Sure thing," Dambree said, reaching down and grabbing a mug. She set it down under the tap and reached back down.

"You see which way he went, cutey pie?" the skinnier one asked.

Dambree pointed with the hand that had been holding onto the tap, pointing out the window. "That way."

They both turned to look.

When they looked back their eyes widened behind their eyeshades. Not just the suddenly ice-cold eyes of the teenage girl, not just the calm way she stood, but at the heavy pistol in her hand with a burning green light on the side that she was looking down the holographic sight of.

Dambree fired twice.

STONE COLD

*"It's all fun and games until you're someone's
idea of fun."* – Black Ear Motto

Dambree had spent two days pouring over the instruction manual for the pistol, learning even how to take it apart to clean it and then put it back together. She had practiced with the different types of sights, learned how to put it on 'safe' and how to change the ammunition types. She'd even used the 'ghost round' feature to practice firing.

She knew it didn't make her an expert. It took her almost two hours to clean it, and she had spent a lot of time figuring out the best type of ammunition to possibly use.

After going over it and talking quietly with Mister Mewmew, she had chosen the one that seemed safest, that wouldn't go clear through a wall, that wouldn't kill six people in a row in a crowd.

Low-V APERS-F-T was her choice.

The letters burned on the side of the pistol with cold dark blue light as she brought the pistol up, the holographic sight, set for a color range she could easily see and her visual acuity, lifted on the top of the heavy black metal weapon.

She had her right foot forward, her left foot back, crouched slightly, her left hand grabbing her right wrist, her left eye closed and her right eye relaxed open. The holographic sight flashed and she tapped the trigger, aiming, as the instructions had advised for multiple targets, at the lower section of 'center mass', moving the pistol to the right and firing as soon as it lined up with 'center mass', her mind empty, clear singing purpose.

You will hurt my littles, went through her mind. She squeezed, not yanked, the firing stud.

From the black warsteel frame of the pistol a tingling burning feeling ran up her arm and she heard it, relived it, flattened her ears at it.

I'M NOT IN HERE WITH YOU, YOU'RE IN HERE WITH ME! the Terran's voice roared out in her head, her shoulder burning from the tingle that tasted like hot copper on her tongue.

The pistol gave two loud THA-WHACK! as the railgun flung it forward and the magnetic coils stabilized the round, imparting a spin on it that used to be accomplished by barrel rifling as well as breaking the magnetic bonds in the round, allowing it to separate according to the data provided by the scope. The round, a two inch long 10mm slice of durachrome, separated along the four lines down the length, turning into sixteen darts spreading out according to the scope's distancer for maximum effectiveness. Each flechette left a streak of light as the tracer, a thin layer of white phosphorous, lit the path of each flechette.

For either of the men, none of that mattered.

All that mattered is sixteen durachrome flechettes, each of them to inches long and 2.5mm thick, some of them tumbling, hit them square. The first one, the one of the left, took it in the lower torso, the tumbling flechettes wreaking havoc.

One exited out his shoulderblade in a spray of gore and bone chips to stick in the door.

The other one took them in the chest, one bouncing off his sternum and ripping away half of his lower jaw.

Both went down in a spray of blood and gore.

Dambree inhaled sharply, having exhaled and stopped herself from inhaling just like she had practiced.

She swallowed thickly then slid the pistol into the holster before picking up her mug and draining half of the thick dark fizzybrew in one long convulsive swallow. She wiped the foam from her upper lip's fur and turned to look at the two men.

One was still moving. The one she'd shot first. He was weakly moving his arms, trying to hold onto his stomach, one leg kicking, and his mouth was opening and closing.

Dambree sighed. She knew what she had to do.

They might be infected with something, that's why they're being disgusting, she thought, taking another drink off her fizzybrew. She looked around until she saw what she needed.

Fishing jumpsuit. Perfect. The dark green cloth would keep blood and water from getting to her clothing.

Work gloves. Perfect, prevent her from nicking her hand and getting blood in it. She'd learned how important that was in health class.

A grav-ski mask. It would protect her face, keep her from getting anything in her mouth, and shield her eyes. Used for high wind and water spray, it was perfect.

She walked over, picking up each item and carrying it back to counter. She got dressed, sealing the fishing jumpsuit and making sure the mask was properly set. She buckled the LawSec belt over the thick jumpsuit, adjusting it for a moment, then added one of the heavy knives the shelf claimed were "wilderness survival hiking knives" and clipped the sheathe to the belt.

Then she turned back to the two men.

Dambree had hoped the man would just die, but he was still moaning and moving around. There was a neural pistol near his hand and Dambree walked over and kicked it out of the way. He looked up at her and squinted his eyes in hate.

"Brat. Stupid brat," he whispered.

Dambree just turned around and walked over, getting what she needed.

She walked back and looked down at him.

"Stupid slut," he whispered.

Dambree hit him in the face with the long-handled axe.

The second hit and he stopped moving. She had to put one foot on his chest to yank the axe free, splattering herself and the door. She was breathing heavy, adrenaline spiking through her system, when she heard it.

"What's going on in there?" a man's voice whispered from the other side of the door. "Are you guys OK?"

She stepped back, her stomach twisting for a second as she realized it was an adult.

The door opened to reveal a man dressed in a LawSec uniform, the front dark with old, dried blood. He had a neural pistol in his hand, eyeshades on, and heavy boots. He was taller than her, wider than her, and she knew he was stronger than her.

He could hurt her.

He stood there, one hand on the handle of the door, the other holding tight to the neural pistol. He hadn't been sure what had happened in there, there were just two loud noises, then nothing. He'd gotten nervous, waiting in front of the LawSec cruiser they'd stolen the day before, so he'd come up to see if they were just in there messing around.

Now he was staring at the figure in front of him. Bulky, with a LawSec belt around their waist, heavy boots, farmer's boots, on their feet. They wore heavy work gloves and dark green coveralls splattered with blood.

With an axe in their hands.

But that wasn't the worst.

They had on a white mask with three thin red stripes, spattered with blood, with dark black holes for eyes.

Dambree let go of the axe, her hand going to the pistol. It took two tugs to get it free, and Dambree was sure the entire time that he was going to raise the neural pistol and shoot her or pull the knife from his belt and stab her, or knock her down to step on her ears till she did what he wanted her to do.

He watched the figure in front of him cock their head slightly. One hand let go of the axe handle and slowly moved to the pistol, the hand resting there.

His bladder let go.

This wasn't like chasing down fleeing people and having some fun.

He didn't know what this was, but it wasn't fun.

The bulky gloved hand slowly pulled the heavy black pistol free. It wasn't like the neural pistols, it looked heavy, blocky, lethal, and the green light burned with a sullen anger.

He dropped the pistol and turned to run, starting to sob.

This wasn't fun. This wasn't fun at all.

Dambree didn't know if he was running for help or not.

She couldn't take the chance.

The pistol lined up with her eye, the holographic sight flashed, and she tapped the trigger. The ear protection in the grav-skiing mask muted the KA-WHACK of the pistol.

The flechettes threw him off his feet, he slid face down in the mud, head first, until he thudded against the tire of the Law-Sec Country Cruiser and came to a stop.

Dambree stepped up and into the doorframe, dragging the axe with one hand, looking around. The grav-ski mask had light enhancement, making the night bright as day, with a color-pallet replacement making everything full color.

Another male was standing beside the second vehicle, his eyes wide.

For nearly three days they'd done what they wanted. The thirst, the never-ending thirst, driving them on, the headaches from the screaming hammering their thoughts, making it so they could do whatever they wanted to whomever they wanted.

They'd decided to check the campground, see if anyone was there, and have a little fun with them.

Staring at the figure in the doorway, dragging an axe behind them, staring at him from behind a white mask, he realized something terrible.

Someone else could have fun with him.

He squealed, his ears going straight up, and he started to hold his hands out, unaware he had a neural pistol still held in one hand.

Dambree stepped out into the rain, walking to the side, the pistol heavy in her hand. It felt like it was snarling, angry somehow.

You want to hurt my littles, she thought to herself, her thoughts as cold and sharp as the axe-blade she was dragging through the cold mud.

He was beyond speech, part of him wondering why it was fair that after three days of fun, he had to come across some maniac in a mask. Why was it fair? He'd only been having fun.

The thirst roared up and he licked his lips.

"You don't wanna hurt me," he said.

The figure stopped, staring through the black eye holes of the mask.

"Come on, I didn't do anything to you," he said. He licked his lips. "I mean, if you found a cutie-pie somewhere, I'm not going to try to take it."

The figure raised an arm, something black and blocky he couldn't quite make out held in the fist.

Dambree pulled the trigger again.

Just go away and leave us alone, she thought as the body fell to the ground, the chest blown apart by the flechettes, burning white in the wounds from the white phosphorus.

She slumped slightly, slowly holstering the pistol. She heft the axe and walked over to each body, hitting them twice in the face.

Always make sure you finish them off. Nothing is more dangerous than a wounded animal, she heard in her brain.

She put all four bodies in the same LawSec car and drove it to a nearby cabin, parking it. She turned on the lights, including the spotlights, rolled up the windows, turned on the heater, locked the doors, and walked away. The other LawSec vehicle she parked next to the first, repeating it. She used the mag-lock key to check the trunks, but they were empty.

Her backpack was right where she left it. She shrugged into it and stepped out into the rain, carefully closing the door behind her.

Dambree knew she'd need the axe to the cut the wood in the shed but it was heavy in her arms. She pushed up the mask so she could drink the fizzybrew in her off hand, walking through the dark of the night, through the rain, back to the little cabin.

Mister Mewmew was waiting inside and watched as she slowly undressed. He rubbed against her ankles when she took off her boots and socks and sat on the couch wiggling her toes.

"I brought back stuff, Mister Mewmew," she said, cracking open a bottle of fizzybrew.

Mister Mewmew made the :-) sign on his head.

"There were some bad people who wanted to hurt me."

:-(

"I made sure they couldn't hurt Tru, Elu, and Nee," she said softly. She slid the pistol out of the holster and set it on the coffee table. "I made sure they couldn't hurt anyone ever again."

:-(

She took a long drink and looked at the little furry robot. "Do you still love me, Mister Mewmew?"

<3

"I'm glad. I don't know if I do any more," Dambree looked down at her bare feet, the fur looking crinkled and rough. "But I love you too, Mister Mewmew."

Mister Mewmew sat and watched Dambree as she slowly worked her way through the fizzybrew, her eyes getting heavier and heavier, until she finally went to sleep.

"Bree, Nee ate another bug," Elu said from the other side of the sheet that Dambree had hung up.

Dambree didn't look away from where she was rubbing shampoo into Tru's fur while Tru sat in the steaming hot water in the large plasteel tub.

"She'll be fine," Dambree said.

"Eww, I can see the legs poking out of her mouth," Elu said.

"She'll be fine," Dambree said, scrubbing a particularly stubborn patch of grime. Two days of being in the basement had left grime all over her siblings.

"When we're done I get to keep one of the new dataslates for just me?" Tru asked.

"Yup. But you have to play games with Mister Mewmew for at least three hours each day," Dambree said. "And do your chores."

"I don't like chores," Tru said.

"I know," Dambree said, pulling Tru's ear against her head so she could wipe down the long interior.

"Do I have to do them?" Tru asked.

"Do you want to eat?" Dambree said, moving to the other

ear.

"Yeah."

"Then you have to do your chores or nobody eats. Close your eyes," Dambree said. She scooped out hot water with the big measuring cup and poured it over her little sister's head, making sure to rinse her ears.

"All right, all done. Wrap up in the towel, go in the bedroom and dry off then get dressed," Dambree said.

Tru got out, grabbing the swimming towel and wrapping it around herself. Dambree took a second to realize that the pictures on the towel were of a popular Hesstlin singer that she'd been nearly obsessed by.

But that was before the Slorpys came.

"Come on, Elu, time for your bath," Dambree said.

"But you're a girl," Elu protested.

"I know," Dambree said. "Did momma bathe you?"

"Well, not often. I'm too old," Elu said.

"That was before the Slorpys came and the rain turned black. Mister Mewmew wants me to rub this shampoo all over, it's medicine," Dambree sighed.

"Promise you won't peek?" Elu said.

"Lu, I have to make sure you don't have any hurties from the black rain or the big explosions from the fighting. Do you want your peepee to shrivel up and fall off?" Dambree asked, falling back on a half-threat.

"No!"

"Then you have to have me make sure you're all right and rub this shampoo into you," she sighed. "You can do your own peepee when I'm done like Tru did hers before I came in. I'll leave so you can."

"OK," Elu said. "It's embarrassing for girls to see me naked."

"I know. I'm not a girl any more," she said the last part softly as Mister Mewmew horked up more shampoo into the dish.

"Ew! Nee ate another bug!"

"She's fine."

She knew why her mom sometimes seemed so tired.

"Do we have to stay here?" Tru asked as she helped carry the last of the supplies they taken from the store out of the trunk and into the cabin. They'd taken everything, right down to the last fishing lure and roll of toilet paper in the bathroom.

A group of Terran jets roared by, almost touching the trees, right after she finished speaking.

"Yes. As long as we have to until we don't hear..." Dambree waiting a moment.

Explosions echoed off the granite ridges of the mountain on the other side of the lake, slapping against the water of the lake, then booming around them.

"...that any more," Dambree finished.

"I'm scared," Tru said.

"I know," Dambree said.

"Momma and daddy wouldn't like me shooting a gun," Elu said, looking nervously at the long gun in his hands. Dambree had looked it up, it was called a shotgun according to the file Mister Mewmew had put in the dataslate.

"Well, they're dead," Dambree said harshly.

Elu's lower lip and his nose twitched, his ears trembled, and his eyes glittered.

But he didn't cry.

Dambree looked over at Tru, just to check on her youngest siblings. Punee was sitting on Tru's lap, chewing on a sucky, glaring at everyone with her amber eyes. She'd been grouchy since she'd managed to pull herself up on her feet and reach for the pistol only for Dambree to pick it up and move it over to the counter.

Off in the distance the roar of artillery fire slamming into the ground echoed off the mountain.

Dambree watched Tru identify which plants were poisonous, which plants were edible, and which plants were just plants. Elu was following the instructions on his dataslate for cleaning the shotgun, making sure the barrel was pointed away from everyone.

Dambree had already smacked him hard for not paying attention.

It's not fair. They should be in school, playing with friends, not having their crazy older sister make them take tests from a Camping 4 NOObz book, she thought to herself.

Some kind of sixth sense she'd developed warned her and she turned in time to see Punee pulled herself up, her little knees and hocks trembling, and slap her hand on the coffee table by the couch. When she realized what she wanted wasn't there she glared at Dambree.

"I know," Dambree chuckled, patting where the pistol rode in the holster. "Good try, though. Good girl."

Punee just glared.

Outside aircraft roared overhead.

The snow whispered as it fell from the sky, piling up on the ground. Her breath steamed in front of her as she tromped from the lakeside toward the hidden cabin. She was bundled up for the cold, having followed the advice in books and her companion.

Mister Mewmew jumped through the snow with her, his tail flicking back and forth as he would vanish into the snow then explode out in a spray of white, then vanish again.

Dambree went around the corner of the rocks, sighing with pleasure as she saw the cabin. The windows were dark, but that was to be expected with the heavy curtains over the glass. Smoke came from the chimney, but that was to be expected. She had a tiny fusion reactor, but preferred not to turn it on in case any of the slorpies were around.

She stopped outside the door, brushing off her clothing, then hurried inside, letting Mister Mewmew slide in before shutting the door and putting the blanket back over it.

It was warm in the cabin and Dambree felt a sudden fatigue come over her.

Nee crawled across the clean wooden floor, kicking with her little feet, her hocks and knees flexing like they should, getting stronger every day, until she reached Dambree. Dambree looked down at her baby sister as the infant grabbed tightly onto Dambree's heavy pants and slowly, tremblingly, pulled herself to her feet, ankles, hocks, and knees shaking. She reached up and smacked Dambree's knee, obviously trying to reach up.

"Not quite big enough, are you?" Dambree chuckled, resting her hand on the heavy Terran soldier's pistol that rode in a holster on hip. "Good girl to stand. Good girl, Punee."

Punee glared with her beautiful amber eyes and dropped back down to her hands and knees, crawling back over to the couch.

"Any problems?" Dambree asked, kneeling down and undoing the laces on her heavy boots.

"Nee at a bug," Dambree's little sister Tru said as Dambree got off the boots.

"Tough shit for the bug, I guess," Dambree said. She flexed her toes and her mid-foot joint and sighed.

"Tru called me a stupid-head," Elu, her little brother, said accusingly as Dambree walked through the cabin's main room.

"Don't call your brother stupid," Dambree said, leaning over and smacking her sister across the back of the head.

"Ew, those fish are stinky," Tru said.

"You won't say that after I cook them," Dambree said. She set the fish on the counter and reached out and got a little rod that Mister Mewmew had given her. She tapped the end, then slid the rod into the gills of each fish.

After a second or two a little LED turned green and she'd go to the next fish.

None of them had atom smasher sickness.

She smiled to herself as she got out the heavy pan and put it on the stove. She checked the bottom door and saw that the coals were still burning.

"Thank you for making sure the stove didn't go out today, Elu," Dambree said, opening the cold box and pulling a bottle of fizzybrew out.

"I don't want to eat cold food from a can again," Elu said as

Dambree took a deep drink off the bottle.

Punee managed to pull herself up and look at the low table next to the couch, smacking it with her little hand. When she saw that what she was after was missing she glared at Dambree.

"Sorry, Nee, it's not for babies," Dambree chuckled, putting her hand on the pistol. "Good girl to stand up, though."

Nee just glared and sat down.

Dambree smiled as she started following the instructions on how to clean and prepare fish for eating.

It was warm in the cabin.

And the echoing boom of the war was just a reminder to stay where they were.

Dambree wasn't even aware she was humming a song as she made her little brother and sisters a dinner of fried fish, vegetables, and a self-heat pack of starches.

Her day had gone so good that she just laughed when Punee tried to bite her when she was feeding her starchy goop.

"I love you," she said to the baby. She looked at her little brother and sister. "I love you."

NOT WITH A BANG
BUT A THWACK

"Even the Detainee won't recognize him now." –
Mike Hammer, Pre-Diaspora Detective

It drifted through the snowy forest, for the first time in its hundreds of thousands of years of life shielding and masking its psionic powers, suppressing its aura, holding all of its psychic abilities deep inside of itself. It had to rely on its eyes, which watered painfully in the moonlit night even though thick clouds covered the moon. It drifted, unwilling to walk. No, it would rather die than walk like a slave race.

It knew if it could get far enough away from the howling and snarling feral intelligences that had harried it, that had destroyed the invasion, that had had the audacity to actually assault its perfection with their rude limbs, it could open up a link to its others. Once a link was established it could guide others through the dark dimension that they traveled via wormhole.

It refused to flee this planet. It had been granted the stellar system and all within it. It had chosen the stellar system carefully. An entire species of peaceful creatures who could be harvested, farmed, and forced to serve as was proper.

Instead the foul primates just kept swarming, kept denying its greatness.

It drifted around a crude ground vehicle, ignoring the corpses inside.

It refused to admit to the pain, its head ached from the gibbering maddened screams emanating from the primate's brains. It drifted through the forest, trying to enjoy the serenity of the darkness, the cold, and the snow.

It was glad that the hated stellar mass was hidden from view. It had not been properly adjusted to proper light and size, instead it was small, yellow, wastefully energetic.

It saw the rippling shimmer of free standing liquid dihydrogen-monoxide and moved toward it. It would use the liquid to ground out the snarling growling screaming of the primates and center itself.

Maybe then it could...

...

...

it drifted to a stop. It could sense a mind. Fresh, undamaged by the psychic screams of the fighting. The mind's feather light trace tasted youthful, full of potential and latent power.

It changed direction, the sense of the unshielded mind vanishing and reappearing strangely. When it rounded a bend, it understood.

The rock was full of heavy elements and hid a small rude dwelling.

Inside it could feel the minds burning brightly and one enter the crude building.

Feeling a close approximation to pleasure and anticipation it glided toward the domicile with the lit viewing portals.

"Nee ate another bug," Elu said from the couch.

"She's fine," Dambree said, kicking the back door shut. She had cut firewood in her arms that she dropped in the wood box next to the stove. She sighed, shrugging out of her jacket and setting it on the hook, then tugged off her boots.

She could see Elu and Tru sitting at the table, doing lessons from Mister Mewmew that Mister Daisy had given him. Nee was sitting over by the gap in the floorboards that led under the house, chewing away, two bug legs sticking out of her mouth. She was drooling, a happy expression on her face, her ears straight up, and her beautiful amber eyes watching Dambree.

Dambree walked in, sighing, and undid the gunbelt. She

hung up the belt and put the heavy pistol on the end table before sitting down. Mister Mewmew jumped up and on her lap, purring softly. Dambree saw Nee put her hands down and start to crawl, chewing on the bug.

Dambree sighed. Life was...

the door crashed open and Dambree stood up, reaching for the pistol.

"UNLOCK!" she yelled, leaning for it.

FTHWOOP

Dambree tumbled to the floor, her mind fuzzy. Elu and Tru fell from their chairs, stunned, Elu crying out in pain and fear. Dambree tried to move, tried to get up, but her body was nothing but a numb tingling and burning mass.

She heard Mister Mewmew snarl.

FTHWOOP

The snarl cut off and Mister Mewmew fell on the floor in front of Dambree's eyes. As she watched Mister Mewmew's body turned silver and then began to ooze into a puddle around a small skeleton-like robot.

There was silence in the cabin, except for a light pitterpat behind the couch, between the couch and the kitchen table.

She was suddenly yanked up, held in mid-air.

Dambree wished that she could scream.

The creature was disgusting. Dark purple flesh that glistened with oil or slime, the flesh looking like the tentacle things she'd seen in aquariums on field trips. It had a large pointed head, huge white eyes, and tentacles on the lower third of its face. It wore an iridescent robe that was scorched in places and stained with dark patches, and it rode on a disk of swirling purple energy.

It lifted up one many fingered hand and twitched its fingers.

Dambree felt her ears get pushed back, felt like something was touching her mind, caressing it.

Her fur stood up as it felt like a long wet tongue licked her brain inside her skull.

The tentacles parted, revealing a tightly puckered sphincter. Dambree wished, again, that she could scream, but she could barely breathe, just raggedly sporadic inhalations and exhalations. The sphincter opened wide, revealing a raw dark purple maw with row after row of triangular teeth in a spiral that led to the back of the throat.

She felt pressure on her ears, felt like her ears were being pulled apart.

Her skin split between her ears and she knew what it was doing.

It was peeling the skin from her head.

It was drooling, thick ropes of slime, the teeth moving inside the mouth.

Dambree tried to scream again as it started to lean forward.

THWACK!

The whole upper half of the being vanished in a spray of purple mist and scraps of tissue as Punee finally managed to get what she had been after for months, the kick of the heavy pistol slamming her down on her butt as her sister fell to the ground and took a deep whooping breath as her little brother and little sister clumsily got up and rushed toward her and her baby sister cried in pain and fear, surprised by the kick, the noise, and landing on her butt.

She glared at Dambree with her amber eyes as if it was her sister's fault.

RESCUE ATTEMPT

"If you fuck with the universe, it fucks back." - Pre-Diaspora Astrophysicist.

"I don't have to explain shit." - Universe-chan, Meme of 2nd Millennia Post-Diaspora

"If you mess with time, the universe brings in all the dicks. Dicks until the end of time." - Temporal Researcher, unknown era

"If God plays dice, they're loaded." - Alberto Einstein, Pre-Diaspora Physicist

"If you make the universe angry, it will crush you like a bug. The problem is, the Universe is always annoyed." - Unknown

"WHEEEE!" - Terran Descent Humanity

There are always military theorists who will espouse their pet theories to anyone who will listen.

From those who said that tanks spelled the end of infantry to those who claimed drones spelled the end of tanks to those who stated that the nanoforge ended the need for logistics lines at all, everyone all has their pet theories.

Of course, they usually espouse them from the comfort of their lavish homes or from far back from the front lines where any soldier will tell you the one simple fact:

Kill the enemy, break his shit, and convince his population to end the fight.

Hesstla was a small planet, only 80% the size of Earth, originally populated by a small people only a meter and a half high compared to the Terran and Treana'ad and Rigellian two to three meters. They were covered in soft fur, they had little whiskers, they had long sensitive ears, and their legs had a hock joint.

The first few Terrans who met them said that they looked

like someone taught a bunny to walk upright.

They were a peaceful people. When they had discovered the radio they had rapidly progressed to the Information Age and had been edging on the Atomic Age.

The Lanaktallan had arrived only two hundred years after the people of Hesstla had discovered the radio. The people of Hesstla had found out that their planet was claimed by a MegaCorp over a million years before the Hesstlan people had discovered fire.

To their credit, they tried to fight.

It took the Lanaktallan nearly twenty years to put down the last of the rebellion.

Four hundred years of debt peonage had followed. Crushing poverty, their resources exploited, their cities rebuilt for Lanaktallan comfort and aesthetics, their planet no longer alone.

Then had come the Precursor Autonomous War Machines.

They had come into the system, most of them damaged, fleeing a greater threat. They had destroyed the Lanaktallan military forces and seized the extraction and refining facilities. They had landed mechanical horrors to destroy those that lived on the modest little planet.

As the first machine landed the entire population of Hesstla had heard the roar.

HEAVY METAL INCOMING!

The foe that the Autonomous War Machines were fleeing was arriving.

The Hesstla, running and hiding, had frozen. A prey's response to the roar of a predator.

Then the predators had arrived.

HEAVY METAL IS HERE!

The Autonomous War Machines had screamed at the foe that was harrying them.

THERE IS ONLY ENOUGH FOR ONE!

The Hesstlan people had huddled down, scurrying to basements, storm shelters, underground parking garages, wherever they could take shelter surrounded by their own kind.

The predators screamed back.

THEN DIE ALONE!

In less than a week it was over. The AWM's that did not flee, pursued by the predators, were destroyed.

The Lanaktallan returned or left their own shelters, immediately demanding that the new people, the predators, leave the planet, that it was the Unified Neo-Sapient Council's property and property of the corporations.

The predators had said one simple line: "Make me."

The Lanaktallan had fled, promising dire retribution, telling the Hesstla people that the predators would destroy them.

Two years had passed. The damage was repaired. The Hesstlan people consulted about what they wished, and the Terrans had built several military bases and helped the Hesstlan people build orbital structures.

Then the newest ones had arrived.

Without warning.

But still with a scream that told the Hesstlan people where they stood.

YOU BELONG TO US!

The predators, those confusing chaotic primates, the Terran Descent Humans, and their allies, had raised up their voices as one to the newcomers.

EAT A DICK!

The fighting had been fierce. Atomic weapons had been used. Cities reduced to rubble. Farms burnt to the ground. The newcomers had swarmed Hesstla, a seemingly endless stream of enemies that had pushed the Hesstlan people to the brink.

The Terrans and their allies had pushed back.

Step by bloody step they pushed the newcomers, the Slorpies, back even as they destroyed them.

Four months of bitter fighting on the ground and, somehow, seventy-five *years* in orbit, the Terrans had thrown themselves at the enemy guns, had smashed their machines, had raised their voices in defiance.

EAT A DICK!

On the afternoon of the first month of the year, on the nineteenth day, at approximately 1750 Hours (Out of 28) Local Time, the last of the newcomers was finished off by a single shot from a pistol's accidental discharge.

The war...

...was over.

Not that the fighting was over. That raged on. The newcomers Autonomous War Machines kept fighting, even without supervision, attempting to open up a portal to bring in reinforcements. To harvest the living brains of the people of Hesstla in order to generate enough psychic energy to open a gate to allow more of the newcomer race, the Slorpies, to enter the battle and change the course of history.

The only problem was, for the first time in a hundred million years, the Slorpies were facing a race that did not crumble before psychic assaults. That replied to the cold logic of their psychic powers with feral screams of red hot rage.

In orbit, the fighting came to a slow stop. Even with the loss of the Black Fleet, the remaining Terran vessels managed to smash the enemy from the skies. On the ground, even with the loss of the Enraged Ones, the ground forces managed to rally, managed to deny the Slorpie machines landing zones, scattering their forces into packets and smidgens. To jawnconnor them into nothing more than smashed junk.

Not without a price.

There was valor and sacrifice. Too much to count.

From a Terran that gave his life to stop the Slorpie machines from getting into a shelter to the Telkan who stood defiant at the gate of a hospital base to the black Mantid fire team that had boarded a Slorpie command and control AWM to destroy the linked brains at the cost of their own lives.

There was tragedy too. Too much to count.

There always is in war.

But there is always hope. Perhaps small and flickering, but still hope.

Elu watched as the door opened after the two-three-two knock. He had covered the shotgun with a cloth, making sure it was pushed back to where Nee couldn't reach it, when the knock had come. Still, it was close enough for him to grab if he needed to.

His sister, Dambree, came inside, quickly turning to close the door behind her and block out the snow and wind.

She was wearing heavy boots, thick coveralls, and a gravskiiing mask to protect her face from the cold weather outside. She wore a thick leather belt with a heavy Terran pistol in a holster. In one hand she held winter tubers, in the other hand she had four fish on a lead. She moved into the kitchen, setting the fish in the sink and the tubers on the counter, then took off her thick gloves and stripped off her mask.

Elu saw the scar on his sister's head and winced. It had been a month since that *thing* had come in to attack them. It had somehow split his sister's skin open from right between her eyes, up over her head between her ears, and halfway down the back of her head. The scar was an angry upraised purple thing.

And a reminder of why they stayed in their little cabin.

"Gunka roots and fish for dinner tonight," Dambree said, taking the pistol out of the holster. "Lock," she ordered.

The telltales on the pistol switched from green to red.

"Can we have the roots fried?" Tru, Elu's sister, asked hopefully. "I like them best when they're fried."

"I know. That's up to you. It's your turn to cook dinner," Dambree said, taking off the belt. She moved back to the doorway. "It's snowing again. It's going to be a long winter."

The roar of jets went by overhead and off in the distance.

"Fried roots and baked fish," Tru said, standing up from the couch.

Mister Mewmew looked up from his little nest and made a plaintive complaining sound.

"Everyone's OK, Mister Mewmew," Dambree said, hanging up the mask, her gloves, and starting to strip off the coveralls.

Mister Mewmew laid back down in his nest, flashing a ":-)"

on the display on his forehead.

Dambree went into the bedroom and changed out of her heavy outside clothing, putting on a dress and changing her shoes. She came back out and put her boots next to the door, the heavy leather belt acting as a belt or sash to her dress.

The pistol went back in the holster.

"How's Nee?" Dambree asked.

"Sleeping," Tru said, sharpening the knife and trying to decide whether she wanted to slice up the tubers first or clean and bone the fish.

"She's cranky," Elu said helpfully, moving over and sitting down on the couch. He reached over and petted Mister Mewmew, who began to rumble happily.

"I know. Growing does that to you," Dambree said. She opened the cold box and pulled out a fizzybrew, cracking it open and taking a long drink before sitting down. "Lake's almost completely covered with ice."

Elu felt a little despair. He missed his friends, missed school.

Missed his parents.

Mister Mewmew opened his eye, the other one always stayed closed, and rubbed his head against Elu's hand to ease the young Hesstlan's stress.

More jets roared by overhead.

"Where will we live when that stops?" Elu asked quietly. His sister Dambree didn't like to talk about the future, just saying none of it mattered till those noises stopped.

Dambree stared at the lip of the fizzybrew bottle for a long moment.

"I don't know," she sighed. She took another drink. "Part of me thinks I'll just stay right here, in this little cabin, for the rest of my life," she said softly. "People in charge will probably want us to leave, go to a camp or a foster home."

"I want to stay here, with you," Tru said, slicing open the belly of the first fish.

"I know," Dambree said. She gave another deep sigh and

took a long pull off the bottle. "I want you to too."

Elu moved over and opened the curtain a tiny bit, staring outside. He could see the markings from the snowshoes his sister had worn on the snow but the tracks were starting to disappear as more snow came down to add more to the waist high snow.

At least it was white and not gray or black.

"Remember when we used to play in the snow," Elu said quietly.

"We'd make snowmen and throw snowballs," Tru said, smiling. "We'd go to Aunt Fenn's house and have a snowball fight with Ultrek and Ellaf and..."

Tru's smile vanished and she sniffled. "I miss Aunt Fenn."

"I know," Dambree said. "I do too."

"I wish we could go back to how it was before the gross things came," Tru said softly, staring at the fish as she sliced away the flesh.

"I know, but we can't. Babies wish," Dambree said. She got up, drinking down the last of the fizzybrew. She dropped the empty in the garbage and grabbed another. She sat back down. "Babies wish, we're not babies any more."

Mister Mewmew jumped down off the couch, staggering slightly, then limped over to Dambree, putting his front paws on her leg and meowing. Dambree lifted him up and set him in her lap, petting him with long strokes.

Mister Mewmew didn't walk or jump so well since the Slorpie had come in the house.

She could still remember it. The horror of not being able to move, her brother and sister crying out in pain and confusion. The way the Slorpie had lifted her up, had started to peel open her head, had *touched* her brain somehow with a long and disgusting tongue.

Dambree closed her eyes tightly and shuddered, then took a long drink off of her fizzybrew.

At least her headaches had slowly eased up.

She sat in the chair, feeling tired, closing her eyes. She sipped at her fizzybrew without opening her eyes, even when she heard Tru start to fry the fish and tubers. She wasn't as tired as she had been, but she still got tired easily and the effort to catch fish wasn't as easy as it had been.

Her eyes opened when she heard it. The sound of aircraft outside. It wasn't flying by but instead was getting louder, changing sounds.

Mister Mewmew looked up as Dambree stood up, setting Mister Mewmew on the ground as she looked at her siblings.

"In the basement, now," Dambree said. While her little brother and sister grabbed their emergency bags and hurried into the basement Dambree put a lid of the pan of frying fish and sliced tuber rounds and moved them off of the heat.

The roar changed pitch, getting softer, but not because it was moving away.

Nee bit her when Dambree grabbed her but Dambree ignored the pain, cradling the toddler as she hurried to the kitchen. Dambree picked up the shotgun and hustled after her brother and sister, closing the basement hatch behind her. She had tacked the carpet to it so it would hide the basement access so now all she could do was hope.

Mister Mewmew was held tightly by Tru as they sat quietly in the basement.

Dambree aimed the shotgun at the opening, moving her finger to take the shotgun from safety mode to killing mode. The button went from red to green, colored plastic instead of lights.

The door opened upstairs and Dambree heard Elu suck in his breath.

"Shh," Dambree said.

There was footsteps upstairs. Strange sounding footsteps. A voice said something that Dambree couldn't make out.

"Someone's in the cabin," Tru whined.

"I know, shh," Dambree said.

There was the noise of a chair scraping on wood.

Dambree moved her finger from beside the trigger to the trigger, putting light pressure on it, pulling it tighter into her shoulder.

"There's a lot of them," Tru said helpfully.

"I know, shh," Dambree said. She could hear that both bedrooms were being searched as well as the front room and the kitchen. She heard the back door open, the little chime she'd rigged up ringing on the door and in the basement.

The footsteps stopped. Complete silence upstairs.

"I'm scared," Elu said, his voice tight.

"I know," Dambree said. She licked her dry lips and wished she could take a drink off her fizzybrew.

The hatch started to lift, hit the chain lock, and stopped.

Dambree's scar ached.

A black segmented and insect looking hand reached in, grabbed the chain, and yanked.

The chain popped free.

Dambree pulled the trigger.

The shotgun roared, blowing off part of the hatch.

"YOU WON'T HURT THEM!" Dambree screamed, ignoring the pain in her shoulder and neck as she pumped the action on the shotgun and stood up. She fired again, into the ceiling, blowing a hole as big as her fist in the wooden floor. She cocked it again, moving up to the base of the stairs.

"KUKLI'S DANGLING WARSTEEL BALLS!" someone yelled when she blew a hole in the floor on the other side of the hatch.

"FOR FUCK'S SAKE, STOP FUCKING SHOOTING!" another voice yelled.

Fuck? Dambree paused.

"Terran Army! Hold your fire," another voice said, much more calm. "Next time, try to make sure people can you hear you call out before you rummage through their house, men."

"Terrans?" Dambree asked, still looking down the barrel at the top of the stairs.

"First Cavalry Division. One of our search and rescue flights saw the smoke from your cabin," the voice said. "How many of you are there?"

"Stop biting me," Tru told Nee.

"Four of us and Mister Mewmew," Dambree said. "I'm coming up. Anything funny and I'll blow you in half."

"I'll bet you will, kid," the voice said.

Dambree slowly walked up the stairs, her finger on the trigger. *Six more shells, counting the one in the chamber. Extras are in the kitchen drawer and on a belt hanging next to the back door.*

At the top she looked around.

Six large figures in black armor were in the room, three of them aiming heavy black rifles at her.

"You're Terrans?"

One of them tapped the side of his helmet and his black faceplate turned clear.

Dambree sagged slightly, lowering the shotgun. "You are."

"So you're the masked killer of Sparkling Lake?" the man asked.

Dambree nodded as she slowly walked over to the table, setting the shotgun down. She sat down and picked up her fizzy-brew and took a drink.

"Yeah," she said. The exhaustion filled her again and she took another drink.

The Terrans looked at each other and the one she could see the face of, that she assumed was a male, looked at her. "We're here to save you."

She took another drink.

"I know," she said, getting up. She moved the pan back to the heat.

The human shuffled for a second. "Do you need assistance?"

Dambree took another drink as she slowly turned and looked at them, looked at the shotgun, then at the Terrans again.

A flight of jets went by overhead.

Dambree jerked her thumb up at the now receding jets. "As long as I hear that, we're staying here."

The human nodded slowly. "Is there anything you need? A doctor to look at that scar?"

Dambree shook her head, backing up to lean against the counter. "Mister Mewmew fixed it up."

"Food? Water? Anything?" the Terran asked.

Dambree shook her head. "No."

"Are you parents still alive?" the Terran asked.

Dambree shook her head. "No. They got shlorped."

"Any relatives alive?" he asked.

She shook her head again. "Probably not."

"I'm supposed to take any unaccompanied children to a refugee center," the Terran said carefully. Dambree wondered why his eyes seemed to glow a cold amber.

"You will try," Dambree said. She could hear the faint roar of approaching aircraft again. "I will not allow anyone to take away my siblings until," the jets roared overhead and receded. "Until I do not hear that any longer."

There was silence for a moment before the human nodded. "We'll drop you a survival pack."

The humans turned and started to leave. The one with the transparent visor waited until they were gone.

"The Terran who that pistol belonged to?" he asked.

"Slorpies got him. Sucked out his brain. He killed the Slorpie from inside of it. He gave me the pistol, told me to save the last four shots for my siblings and myself."

The Terran nodded. After a moment two Terrans came in carrying backpacks. They dropped them on the floor and left.

They hadn't turned their visors clear.

"Good luck, kid," the Terran said, his visor going opaque. "You might be here a long time."

Dambree took a long drink off of her fizzybrew as the Terran left, closing the door behind him.

"I know," she said to the empty cabin.

YOU CAN'T GO HOME AGAIN

PLANET HESSTLA
ONE YEAR AFTER CASE OMAHA - LOCAL
TWO MONTHS AFTER CASE OMAHA - GALACTIC

The darkness was pushed back by the light of the moons streaming down, hitting the snow, and illuminating the entire forest. The night was cold, tiny snowflakes drifting down from the heavy clouds, dancing on the cold wind that rustled trees and bushes. The lake was covered in ice, the same with the wooden dock that extended out over the frozen water.

A hole was chopped in the ice, a figure sat on the end of the dock with a fishing pole in one hand and a can of self-cooling fizzybrew in the other. The figure wore a grav-skiing mask that was undecorated pushed back from its face, was clad in heavy insulated coveralls, with a heavy leather belt around its waist where a bulky and weighty Terran magac pistol rode in a holster.

The face was furry, short soft fur, with a triangular nose and short whiskers.

Dambree took another drink off the fizzybrew as she stared at the night sky, twitching the fishing pole now and then to try to create interest in the lure.

Beside her Mister Mewmew lifted his head, looked at the lake, then curled back up.

"We're a pair, aren't we, Mister Mewmew?" Dambree asked.

Mister Mewmew looked up, a :-) appearing on the black macroplast triangle on his forehead.

"It's been a full month," she said softly.

Mister Mewmew nodded.

"Do you think it's really over?" Dambree asked, finishing off her fizzybrew and putting the empty in her tacklebox. She started winding the reel, pulling up her lure. "It's been a full month," she repeated, staring up at the larger of the two moons, which was full and shining brightly.

Mister Mewmew put up a sigil for a shrug.

"I wish I could stay here, with you, for the rest of my life," Dambree said. She pressed the button beside the reel and the fishing rod clacked as it turned into a short baton.

The memory of beating a boy her age to death with it surged up and she pushed it down, pushed away the horror of how his eyes were surrounded by blackened flesh and bloody tears had run down his cheeks, pushed away how it felt for his hands to paw at her, grabbing at her clothing.

She hung the collapsed fishing rod from her belt, tugged her grav-skiing mask down over her face, then knelt down and closed her heavy tacklebox. She grabbed the line of five fish and the tacklebox and slowly stood up.

When she had first started fishing the tacklebox had been heavy enough she had been forced to set it down several times on the trip from the cabin to the dock. Now she barely noticed the weight.

The snow crunched under her boots as she slowly walked back to the cabin. She passed a burnt out car. Wild animals had gotten at the burnt corpses, leaving nothing behind.

She could remember loading the bodies of the two men who had chased Tru into the car before setting it on fire. The third had escaped and she'd tracked him until he had reached the road before she had given up. She had grabbed a branch and dragged it behind her as she wandered back to her cabin, stopping by other cabins, making sure she erased his footprints.

Dambree was frowning under the mask as she passed by a cabin with broken windows, charred wood around the windows and smoke damage to the siding.

That had been the cabin that had taught her that *nobody* could be trusted. Not kids her age, not adults, not girls, not boys, not men, not women. They had seemed so sad and pathetic, their eyes hadn't been bruised, they didn't weep bloody tears.

They had still tried to take what was Dambree's and hurt those under her care.

"It's been a long year," Dambree said softly. She pushed through the bushes she'd planted in what had been the only road leading to the little cabin off to the side. She'd planted them and made sure they were in the way, concealing the cabin.

Mister Mewmew just made a meow-ing noise.

At the cabin Dambree stomped her boots a few times, knocking the snow off of them. She ignored the fact that Elu was pointing the shotgun at her when she came in. Tru was standing with her back flat against the wall, next to the door, a long-bladed knife in her hand.

Just in case someone tried coming in through the back door while Elutra was 'distracted' by someone coming in the front.

Nee was laying on the couch, covered by a blanket, sleeping with a sucky in her mouth.

Elu put up the shotgun, making sure it was out of reach of Nee and up on the wall-pegs before dropping the decorated cloth over it. Tru moved over and put the knife back on the counter.

Dambree moved over and put the fish in the water filled sink where they drifted to the bottom, only the movement of their gills betraying they were alive.

"I'll make dinner," Dambree said. "We'll have cake for dessert."

Both her siblings were overjoyed at it, even though Dambree could hardly breathe because of the anxious feeling in her chest. She boned and scaled the fish, rolled them in flour and spices, then cooked the strips, serving it up with baked tubers and fresh vegetables.

The cake was the last canned cake they had, thick with frosting and overly sweet after months of eating home-made food.

Dambree waited until after her siblings went to sleep, till Nee was curled up with her sister, sucking her thumb, before lifting the basement hatch.

She went down into the basement with a flash, going back to the 'survival pack' that the military had dropped off a couple of months before. She opened the pack, finding what she was looking for quickly. When she left the basement she checked on her siblings again.

All three were asleep.

Dambree dressed slowly, forgoing the mask, and walked out to where the remains of the car she'd driven, half crazed, through the hellish first days of the Slorpy Invasion.

She swept the snow off the seat where the door was missing, sitting down.

Dambree lifted up the device and turned it on. She'd read all about it on the dataslate.

"civil authorities are confirming that there have been no sightings of Precursor Autonomous War Machines for the last three weeks but urge the population not to grow lax. Report any suspicious activity via text or voice. Do not approach susp..." a female voice said.

Dambree turned the knob on the top, changing the channel. The device started making clicks and beeps with what sounded like parts of words.

"Hello?" Dambree said, pressing the button on the side. "Is there anyone listening?" She let off the button.

"Who is this? This is a restricted military channel," a voice answered. "State your emergency."

"No emergency," Dambree said. She took a deep breath and exhaled it. "I think I'm ready to come back."

Dambree sat on the hood of the car, watching as the heavy grav-lifter, the military markings on it scuffed looking, set down slowly in the small clearing. She could see patched and repaired damage on it, see the weapon pods under the short stubby wings. The craft touched down with a whine that slowly oscillated down to silence. The side door slid open and a Terran in the weird shifting colors clothing jumped out.

"Are you Dambree?" the Terran asked, noticing that the young Hesstlan was holding a Terran magac pistol in one hand.

"Yes," the young female said.

"How many of you are here?" the Terran asked. Dambree wasn't sure, but she thought the Terran might be female.

"Five of us. Me, my younger sister, my little brother, and my youngest sister," Dambree said. She smiled. "And Mister Mewmew."

"There was a scout report that suggested you might have had it a little rough," the Terran said.

Dambree just nodded. "I kept them alive. Does anything else matter?" she asked.

The Terran noticed that the Hesstlan girl sounded much older than her features suggested.

"We found out that you have an aunt and two uncles still alive," the Terran said. "We haven't notified them yet."

"Oh," Dambree said. "I didn't know anyone else from my family had survived."

"Should we contact them?" the Terran asked.

Dambree shook her head. "Not yet."

Dambree stared at the 'striker' as the Terran helped her little sister up into it. Nee was already in a safety seat, gnawing on a biter biscuit and glaring at everyone, Elu was already belted in. Mister Mewmew was in something called a kittykitty cradle which would help him feel better so he didn't limp and could jump better.

"Are you all right?" the Terran female asked.

"Yes," Dambree said softly. She wished she had a fizzybrew.

"It's perfectly safe. Warrant Officer Mukstet is an experienced and very skilled pilot," the Terran said. "It's safe to get in."

"I know," Dambree said, wiping her mouth again. She turned and looked at the little cabin where she'd lived for an entire year.

"It's OK if you feel like you don't want to leave," the Terran said softly. "It's all right to feel that way."

"I know," Dambree said. She dug in her jacket pocket and pulled out one of her last cans of fizzybrew, only one more in her other pocket. She cracked it open, staring at the striker, then turning to stare at the house, then at the lake in the distance.

She took a long drink, the fizzybrew soothing her throat.

"I killed a lot of people," Dambree whispered. "They didn't leave me any choice."

"It's all right," the Terran said. "Bad things happen to good people sometimes."

"I know," Dambree said. She took another drink, her hand going to the butt of her pistol. It had a trigger lock on it, the only way the Terrans would let her carry it onto the striker. She took another drink and stepped forward slowly. She stopped twice more in the five meters to the striker's door to take a drink of her fizzybrew and look back at the little cabin. Finally she got in and let the Terran soldier strap her into the seat.

"Can you leave the door open?" Elu asked, feeling excited at being able to ride in an aircraft.

The striker started up, vibrating, and lifted off.

She didn't realize she was silently crying as she watched the cabin dwindle away.

PAGE SIX OF FIFTEEN

additionally the patient has displayed alcohol dependent symptoms. Review of Purrboi-66231a87's records show that patient used alcoholic drinks to hold off traumatic incident stress syndromes and to self-medicate for traumatic stress disorder.

Patient is withdrawn, speaking infrequently, and shows high signs of social withdrawal and attachment disorder. Patient reports difficultly sleeping, hyper-alertness, as well as high anxiety. Patient has also admitted to homicidal impulses around non-family members. Patient shows neural damage from initial Precursor attack, as well as what appears to be close proximity to hostile life form psychic attack.

Physically, the patient is in good health. Several injuries

will require physical therapy, but no surgical intervention is needed.

RECOMMENDED COURSE OF ACTION

Dambree sat in the chair quietly, her hands folded in her lap. She felt naked without the pistol, without her hand axe, without even a knife in her boot. Of course, she didn't have boots on, not since she'd arrived at the Terran Medical Center. Instead she wore soft shoes that were supposed to be comfortable but felt *wrong* on her feet.

She was comfortable with the Terran soldier standing near her. He had a pistol on his hip, his uniform kept trying to blur in with the wall, and he was large as well as dangerous and competent looking.

He felt comfortable to Dambree.

The doctor entered. A russet Mantid by the name of *Soothes the Pain of the Soul*. She moved up and sat on the bench seat next to Dambree.

"They came as soon as you gave consent to have them notified," *Soothes* said. "They didn't think you were alive."

"I know," Dambree said softly.

Soothes noticed that those two words were often her patient's only reply.

"Are you ready?" *Soothes* asked.

Dambree nodded, wiping her mouth with one soft sleeve.

"She's ready. Send them in," *Soothes* said gently.

Dambree sat perfectly still as her two uncles and her aunt came into the room. Her aunt Fenn ran forward, gathering her up in a hug.

Soothes noticed the pause before Dambree hugged her back. Noticed how Dambree's eyes stayed open, how her right hand rubbed up and down on her aunt's back, stopping between her fifth and sixth rib. Dambree let herself be hugged by her two uncles, repeating the action.

She's finding their hearts, Soothes thought to herself.

"We thought you were dead," Matron Fenn said, sitting

down and taking Dambree's hands.

"I know," Dambree said.

Soothes watched as Dambree's Aunt Fenn kept talking, saying how glad they were that Dambree and her siblings had survived. That when they'd seen the house bombed out they'd fear the worst. *Soothes* noticed that Dambree's demeanor didn't even change when she was informed that five of her cousins had survived.

Soothes wasn't sure about clearing the young Hesstlan woman to leave the hospital, but she had three other patients in Dambree's family to worry about.

Later, at the desk, as she signed the release forms, she watched carefully as Dambree and her three siblings, the one called Tru holding onto the damaged purrboi's crate, she felt a little bit of worry.

Not that her patient was a danger.

But that her family might not understand her any more.

Dambree sat on the edge of the bed, staring at the street outside the window. She was rooming with her cousin Meglee. The room felt closed in, almost claustrophobic after the year spent in the cabin. Outside were ground cars, lights, neon, and flickering holograms slightly disrupted by the drifting snowflakes.

She found she missed the quiet of the woods.

Dambree got up slowly, moving over and standing in front of the window. She put her hand on the smartglass, finding it strange how the windowpane was warm instead of carrying the chill of the winter night.

"Dambree?" her cousin said, rolling over and opening her eyes. The sound of her cousin getting up had woken her up.

"Yes," Dambree said.

Meglee frowned sleepily. "You're naked in front of the window."

"I know," Dambree said softly. "It doesn't matter."

"Oh," Meglee said. She rolled over, pulling her blanket

around her. She yawned. "Good night, Dambree."

"Good night, Meglee," Dambree said.

She stared at the snow drifting down for a long moment, then moved over to the bed. She reached underneath it, getting what she'd hidden there early in the morning before anyone else had woken up. She walked back in front of the window and stared out it.

The fizzybrew can snapped and then hissed when she opened it, the contents cooling almost instantly.

The sound disturbed Meglee enough that she shifted slightly under her blanket.

Dambree just stared at the snow, sipping at the fizzybrew.

They mostly come out at night, she thought to herself, remembering the early weeks of the Slorpy Attack. *Mostly.*

The snow kept its secrets as it drifted down.

ABOUT THE AUTHOR

Ralts Bloodthorne

The Creation Engine, the Wordboi, the Mad Arch-Angel TerraSol. Not even he is sure where all of this is coming from, merely that it pours out from his fingertips in a frenzied rush.